PIECES OF MAGIC

. . . *A beautiful, heart-shaped locket* . . . and a curl that cost grandma more than a lock of hair.

. . . *A rusty old trunk,* a "pig in a poke," purchased sight unseen for fifty cents . . . and holding something other than an imagined treasure.

. . . *A tiny pig* dressed in a baby's clothes . . . until the mother mistakes it for her child.

Laugh, enjoy, and read on. . . . You're never too old for a good story!

More Stories from Grandma's Attic

Arleta Richardson

Chariot Books

MORE STORIES FROM GRANDMA'S ATTIC
Copyright © 1979 David C. Cook Publishing Co.

90 89 88 87 86 15 14

Published by David C. Cook Publishing Co., Elgin, IL 60120

Printed in the United States of America
ISBN: 0-89191-131-6
LC: 78-73125

To Ethel
who knew that I could write these stories
and was so pleased when I did.

GRANDMA'S STORIES

WHEN GRANDMA
WAS YOUNG

Ever wonder what it was like when your grandmother was a little girl? I did. And I was lucky enough to have a grandma who never forgot the fun and laughter of her childhood years.

One hundred years ago! That's when my grandma lived on a little farm in Michigan with her ma and pa and her two brothers, Reuben and Roy.

My trips to grandma's old house were my favorite times. I explored the attic and the root cellar, the barn and the meadow brook—all the places a little girl named Mabel, my grandma, knew and loved.

The attic was dusty and creaky, but what marvelous treasures it contained! A funny-looking wire thing that turned out to be something to wear. A slate and the hard pencil that grandma used to write on it, an ancient trunk filled with quilt pieces, and the button basket, a miracle of mysteries. The old house was really a big storybook.

And those stories became mine as grandma told them to me. I could hear Nellie, the family's gentle horse, *clip-clopping* up the long tree-bordered lane and see a small goat dancing stiff-legged through ma's kitchen. I could enjoy the excitement of a day at the exhibition grounds.

From my grandma I learned the meaning of kindness and compassion. I learned how important prayer is, and how rewarding life can be when it is lived for the Lord.

All of this was possible because I loved to hear stories as much as grandma loved to tell them.

So if you are young enough to appreciate a story—and just about everyone is—come with me to a little farm in Michigan and enjoy the laughter and tears that old farmhouse saw so many years ago. . . .

1

The Nuisance
in Ma's Kitchen

WHEN GRANDMA CALLED from the back-yard, I knew I was in for it. It was her would-you-look-at-this voice, which usually meant I was responsible for something.

"What, grandma?" I asked, once I reached where she was hanging up the washing.

"Would you look at this? I just went into the kitchen for more clothespins, and came back out to find this."

I looked where she was pointing. One of my kittens had crawled into the clothes basket and lay sound asleep on a clean sheet.

"If you're going to have kittens around the

house, you'll have to keep an eye on them. Otherwise, leave them in the barn where they belong. It's hard enough to wash sheets once without doing them over again."

Grandma headed toward the house with the soiled sheet, and I took the kitten back to the barn. But I didn't agree that it belonged there. I would much rather have had the whole family of kittens in the house with me. Later I mentioned this to grandma.

"I know," she said. "I felt the same way when I was your age. If it had been up to me, I would have moved every animal on the place into the house every time it rained or snowed."

"Didn't your folks let any pets in the house?" I asked.

"Most of our animals weren't pets," grandma admitted. "But there were a few times when they were allowed in. If an animal needed special care, it stayed in the kitchen. I really enjoyed those times, especially if it was one I could help with."

"Tell me about one," I said, encouraging her to tell me another story about her childhood.

"I remember one cold spring when pa came in from the barn carrying a tiny goat. . . .

"I'm not sure we can save this one." Pa held the baby goat up for us to see. "The nanny had twins last night, and she'll only let one come near her. I'm afraid this one's almost gone."

Ma agreed and hurried to find an old blanket and a box for a bed. She opened the oven door, put the box on it, and gently took the little goat and laid it on the blanket. It didn't move at all, just lay there barely breathing.

"Oh, ma," I said. "Do you think it will live? Shouldn't we give it something to eat?"

"It's too weak to eat right now," ma replied. "Let it rest and get warm, then we'll try to feed it."

Fortunately it was Saturday, and I didn't have to go to school. I sat on the floor next to the oven and watched the goat. Sometimes it seemed as though it had stopped breathing, and I would call ma to look.

"It's still alive," she assured me. "It just isn't strong enough to move yet. You sit there and watch if you want to, but don't call me again unless it opens its eyes."

When pa and my brothers came in for dinner, Reuben stopped and looked down at the tiny animal. "Doesn't look like much, does it?"

I burst into tears. "It *does* so!" I howled. "It looks just fine! Ma says it's going to open its eyes. Don't discourage it!"

Reuben backed off in surprise, and pa came over to comfort me. "Now, Reuben wasn't trying to harm that goat. He just meant that it doesn't . . . look like a whole lot."

I started to cry again, and ma tried to soothe me. "Crying isn't going to help that goat one bit," she said. "When it gets stronger, it will want something to eat. I'll put some milk on to heat while we have dinner."

I couldn't leave my post long enough to go to the table, so ma let me hold my plate in my lap. I ate dinner watching the goat. Suddenly it quivered and opened its mouth.

"It's moving, ma!" I shouted. "You'd better bring the milk!"

Ma soaked a rag in the milk, and I held it while the little goat ate greedily. By the time it had fallen asleep again, I was convinced that it would be just fine.

And it was. By evening the little goat was standing on its wobbly legs and began to baa loudly for more to eat.

"Pa, maybe you'd better bring its box into my room," I suggested at bedtime.

"Whatever for?" pa asked. "It will keep warm right here by the stove. We'll look after it during the night. Don't worry."

"And we aren't bringing your bed out here," ma added, anticipating my next suggestion. "You'll have enough to do, watching that goat during the day."

Of course, ma was right. As the goat got stronger, he began to look for things to do. At first he was contented to grab anything within reach and pull it. Dish towels, apron strings, and tablecloth corners all fascinated him. I was kept busy trying to move things out of his way.

From the beginning the little goat took a special liking to ma, but she was not flattered.

"I can't move six inches in this kitchen without stumbling over that animal," she sputtered. "He can be sound asleep in his box one minute and sitting on my feet the next. I don't know how much longer I can tolerate him in here."

As it turned out, it wasn't much longer. The next Monday ma prepared to do the washing in the washtub pa had placed on two chairs near the woodpile. Ma always soaked the clothes in cold water first, then transferred them to the boiler on the stove.

I was in my room when I heard her shouting. "Now you put that down! Come back here!"

I ran to the kitchen door and watched as the goat circled the table with one of pa's shirts in his mouth. Ma was right behind him, but he managed to stay a few feet ahead of her.

"Step on the shirt, ma!" I shouted as I ran into the room. "Then he'll have to stop!"

I started around the table the other way, hoping to head him off. But the goat seemed to realize that he was outnumbered, for he suddenly turned and ran toward the chairs that held the washtub.

"Oh, no!" ma cried. "Not that way!"

But it was too late! Tub, water, and clothes splashed to the floor. The goat danced stiff-legged through the soggy mess with a surprised look on his face.

"That's enough!" ma said. "I've had all I need of that goat. Take him out and tie him in the yard, Mabel. Then bring me the mop, please."

I knew better than to say anything, but I was worried about what would happen to the goat. If he couldn't come back in the kitchen, where would he sleep?

Pa had the answer to that. "He'll go to the barn tonight."

"But pa," I protested, "he's too little to sleep in the barn, besides, he'll think we don't like him anymore!"

"He'll think right," ma said. "He's a menace, and he's not staying in my kitchen another day."

"But I like him," I replied. "I feel sorry for him out there alone. If he has to sleep in the barn, let me go out and sleep with him!"

My two brothers looked at me in amazement.

"You?" Roy exclaimed. "You won't even

walk past the barn after dark, let alone go in!"

Everyone knew he was right. I had never been very brave about going outside after dark. But I was more concerned about the little goat than I was about myself.

"I don't care," I said stubbornly. "He'll be scared out there and he's littler than I am."

Ma didn't say anything, probably because she thought I'd change my mind before dark. I didn't though. When pa started for the barn that evening, I was ready to go with him. Ma saw that I was determined, so she brought me a blanket.

"You'd better wrap up in this," she said. "The hay is warm, but it's pretty scratchy."

I took the blanket and followed pa and the goat out to the barn. The more I thought about the long, dark night, the less it seemed like a good idea, but I wasn't going to give in, or admit that I was afraid.

Pa found a good place for me to sleep. "This is nice and soft and out of the draft. You'll be fine here."

I rolled up in the blanket, hugging the goat close to me as I watched pa check the animals. The light from the lantern cast long scary shadows through the barn, and I thought about asking pa if he would stay with me. I knew better, though, and all too soon he was ready to leave.

"Good night, Mabel. Sleep well," he said as he closed the barn door behind him. I doubted that I would sleep at all. If it hadn't been for the goat and my brothers who would laugh at me, I would have returned to the house at once. Instead I closed my eyes tightly and began to say my prayers. In a few moments the barn door opened, and Reuben's voice called to me.

"Mabel," he said, "it's just me." He came over to where I lay, and I saw that he had a blanket under his arm.

"I thought I'd sleep out here tonight, too. I haven't slept in the barn for a long time. You don't mind, do you?"

"Oh, no. That's fine." I turned over and fell asleep at once.

When I awoke in the morning, the goat and Reuben were both gone. Soon I found the goat curled up by his mother.

"Will you be sleeping in the barn again tonight?" ma asked me at breakfast.

"No, I don't think so," I said. "I'll take care of the goat during the day, but I guess his mother can watch him at night. . . ."

Grandma laughed at the memory. "After I grew up, I told Reuben how grateful I was that he came out to stay with me. I wonder how my family ever put up with all my foolishness."

Grandma went back into the house, and I wandered out to the barn to see the little kittens. I decided I wouldn't be brave enough to spend the night there—even with a big brother to keep me company!

2

Grandma's Sampler

"SOMETHING IS WRONG with this, grandma," I said. "It doesn't have as many stitches as I started out with."

Grandma took my knitting and looked at it carefully.

"You dropped a stitch back here," she said, and using a crochet hook, she worked the missing stitch back up to the needle.

"It's easier to pick up a stitch as soon as it's dropped than it is to go back and get it later. Sometimes you have to take your work out all the way back to the mistake."

Grandma handed the knitting back to me

and picked up her own work. "I remember that I never had much patience with doing things over when I was your age. In fact, one time I decided not to bother, and I was sorry about it afterward."

"Were you knitting something?" I asked.

"No," grandma replied. "It was a sampler I was embroidering. It was in the spring, just before school was out. . . .

The teacher had announced early in the year that there would be a contest. Everyone in the room would enter some kind of handwork to be judged by the school-board members the last day of school. The prize would be a book—and we didn't have many books of our own.

I determined that I would win the prize, and announced my intentions at the supper table the very day we found out about the contest.

"I'm going to have a new book the last day of school," I said to the family.

"You are?" pa said. "Are you saving all your money to get one?"

Pa knew that I didn't have any money, or any prospects of getting any, so I knew he was just fooling.

I shook my head. "No, I'll get a new book for winning the contest for the best handwork."

"What makes you think you'll win?" Roy asked. "I'm going to enter the contest too, you know."

"Yes, but I'm a more carefuller worker than you are," I replied.

"You mean 'a more careful' worker," ma corrected me. Then she eyed me thoughtfully. "On the other hand, you aren't the most careful worker I've ever seen."

"I will be this time," I said confidently. "I won't hurry, and I'll take lots of pains to do it just right. And besides, I already prayed about it. I asked God to let me win."

This seemed to settle the matter for me. Since I knew the Lord answered prayer, I had no question about winning. Even when pa reminded me that God wasn't going to do the work for me, I was still sure I would win.

The next day Sarah Jane and I decided that we would enter the sewing division and make a sampler. Between our two homes we would surely find enough bright-colored thread to work with, and a square of white linen was not hard to come by.

"What are you going to say on yours?" Sarah Jane asked.

"I haven't decided yet," I replied. "What are you putting on yours?"

"I think I'll put 'Home is where the heart is' and make a border of hearts and flowers.

Doesn't that sound pretty?"

"Yes, it does," I said. "I think I'd like something about friends on mine."

"How about 'A friend loveth at all times'?" Sarah Jane suggested. "That was our Bible verse last week."

"That's good. I'll use that. We'd better practice on something else first though. The one for the contest has to be perfect."

Sarah Jane agreed, and we began drawing the patterns for our letters and flowers. When we finally had them just right, we carefully transferred the work to the cloth.

In the weeks that followed we used every spare moment we had to embroider our samplers. I did the border first, with little flowers and leaves, and I thought it looked quite pretty. Ma agreed.

"You are doing better than I expected, Mabel," she said. "If you do as well on the words, you may have a chance at winning that book."

"Of course I'll win, ma! Sarah Jane's looks nice, but it's not as smooth as mine. She said so herself."

"Just don't be disappointed if you aren't first," ma warned. "It doesn't pay to be too sure of yourself."

But I *was* sure of myself. I just knew that mine was going to be the best one.

About two weeks before the end of the term, Sarah Jane and I sat on the porch, working on our samplers.

"I have just two more words to do, then my name and the date," I announced, and I spread the sampler out on my lap to inspect it again. Sarah Jane looked at it carefully; then an odd expression came over her face.

"Something is wrong, Mabel," she said.

"There can't be!" I exclaimed. "What is it?"

"I think you spelled *friend* wrong."

Horrified, I looked at the word. Sure enough, I had written "A FREND LOVETH AT . . ."

"Oh, no! What can I do to fix it up?"

"You'll have to take it out, back to there," Sarah Jane said. "There isn't room to squeeze an *i* in without looking funny."

"But I don't have time to take it all out," I cried. "Besides it will leave holes where I sewed it, and that will look worse!"

Sarah Jane was sorry, and so was I. It was either take the stitching all out, and probably not finish in time, or leave it in and hope the judges wouldn't notice. I decided I would have to leave it, but I knew I wouldn't win.

Ma was sympathetic. "I think you should put an *i* in here, even though it looks crowded. That would be better than having the judges believe you thought it was spelled correctly.

As many times as you've looked at that sampler, I can't understand how you missed it."

"That's what Sarah Jane said, too," I replied sadly. "When I looked at it, I just thought how pretty it was. I wasn't expecting anything to be wrong. I did so want to win that book! I was *sure* the Lord would answer my prayers."

"Maybe you should have prayed to do your best rather than to win, Mabel. The Lord is willing to help us, but we need to do all we can with the intelligence he gave us."

I knew ma was right, but I was pretty sad the day I took the sampler to school. The teacher agreed that if it hadn't been for that mistake, it might have been a winner.

The last day of school was exciting, anyway. When the contest winners were announced, Roy was in first place in the wood-carving division with a small squirrel he had whittled.

"You can be the first one to read my book, Mabel," he offered generously. "Maybe next year you can enter again and win your own prize."

"That was a good lesson for me," grandma said. "I was often careless after that, but I was careful not to be quite so positive about what I would do again. And I never blamed the Lord for my mistakes, either!"

times as you've looked at that sam...

3

Mrs. Carter's Fright

"GRANDMA, YOU NEVER TOLD ME you dressed a pig in baby's clothes! What did you do that for?" I asked wondering why my commonsense grandma would do such a thing, even when she was a little girl like me.

"Oh, my friend Sarah Jane and I should have been whipped for that prank! We frightened poor Mrs. Carter nearly out of her senses. If she hadn't been such a kind, forgiving lady, I'm sure we would have been punished severely."

"Tell me what happened, grandma," I begged.

27

"After I get the bread in the oven, we'll sit on the porch. You can help me pick over the beans for supper."

Soon we were seated on the porch, and grandma began. . . .

This story happened right on this porch. At least, most of it did. It was a beautiful day in the spring, shortly after school was over for the year. Sarah Jane and I were wandering about, trying to think of the best way to spend the day. We had about decided on a trip to the woods to look for berries when ma changed our minds.

"Don't go too far from the house, girls," she called. "Mrs. Carter is coming to spend the day sewing, and she's bringing her new baby. I know you'll want to see her."

Of course we did. There weren't a lot of new babies in our community, and Sarah Jane and I both loved them. We even thought Mrs. Carter might let us play with little Lucy. So we hung around the gate and watched the road for the first sight of the Carter's wagon.

Very soon it appeared, and we watched Mr. Carter drive up to the front porch. After helping Mrs. Carter down from the front seat, he went to the back of the wagon and took out a beautiful baby buggy. Sarah Jane and I had never seen one so fine before.

"Oh, Mrs. Carter," I said, "may we push Lucy around in the buggy?"

"We'll be very, very careful," Sarah Jane chimed in.

Mrs. Carter smiled at us. "I don't know why not. Just don't go too far from the house. She should go to sleep soon; then you can put the buggy here in the shade, close to the porch."

She laid the baby down, and after admiring her for a few minutes, we began to push the buggy slowly around the yard.

"Wouldn't it be fun to have a real baby to take care of?" I said.

"Oh, yes!" Sarah Jane replied. "Our dolls are nice, but they don't move around and cry like a baby does."

After what seemed like a very short time, the baby went to sleep. We took a few more turns around the house and even shook the buggy a little to see if she might wake up. Finally we decided to put the buggy in the shade as Mrs. Carter had told us to. Then we sat on the edge of the porch and admired the pretty dress and bonnet the baby wore.

"She looks just like a little doll, doesn't she?" Sarah Jane said. "Your doll, Emily, is just about that size. Shall we get our dolls and play with them?"

I agreed, and we brought our dolls and doll

clothes back out to the porch where we could watch the baby as she slept. After a few minutes, Sarah Jane tired of the dolls.

"I'd rather dress something that moves a little," she said, and then spotting the cat walking across the yard, she suggested, "Maybe we could dress the cat."

"You might be able to put clothes on your cat," I said. "But you'll never get a dress and bonnet on this one. He's awfully particular about what he does."

"I suppose Pep wouldn't like it either," Sarah Jane said, figuring our dog was the next best choice.

"I'm sure of it," I replied. "Besides, his head is too big to fit this bonnet."

We sat for a few moments longer, swinging our feet back and forth, when suddenly a brilliant thought came to me.

"I know! How about one of the new baby pigs in the barn? All they do is sleep, but at least they're alive. Shall we get one?"

"Oh, yes, let's!" Sarah Jane exclaimed. "That would be just right for the doll clothes."

So we hurried out to the barn to pick out the cleanest, pinkest piglet we could find. Sure enough, when we had put the dress on that pig and tied the bonnet under its chin, we had what we thought was the next best thing to a real baby.

"Isn't that cute?" Sarah Jane said. "We should have thought of this before." She eyed the buggy, which little Lucy was sleeping in. "I think we should take our baby for a ride."

"We can't put the pig in with Mrs. Carter's baby!" I protested. "She wouldn't like that. Besides, Lucy's still asleep. We might wake her up."

Sarah Jane thought that over. "Why don't you put the baby on your bed to sleep while we take the pig for a ride? Mrs. Carter wouldn't care if you did that."

"OK, she'll be comfortable there." I lifted the baby carefully from the buggy, and with Sarah Jane opening the doors for me, I tiptoed quietly up to my room and put Lucy down on my bed.

"You'd better put her right in the middle so she won't roll off," Sarah Jane suggested.

"She's not big enough to roll over," I said, but I put her as close to the center of the bed as I could and covered her with a blanket. Then we tiptoed out and closed the door.

"There," Sarah Jane said. "She'll probably sleep all morning. Let's take the pig for a ride."

So we ran back outside, put the pig in the buggy, and covered it with a doll blanket. It promptly fell asleep, and we had a great time pretending to be fine ladies strolling through town with their beautiful baby.

Very shortly ma came to the kitchen door. "Girls, it would be nice if you would run to the woods and gather some berries for dinner. It won't be long until it's time to eat. Is the baby still asleep?"

"Yes, ma," I replied. "She's asleep."

"Good. Be sure to leave the buggy in the shade. This small bucket should hold enough berries," she said as she handed us a container.

There was nothing for us to do but take the bucket and start for the woods.

"We'd better hurry," I said, realizing what might happen if we were gone too long.

We picked the berries as fast as we could, not even stopping to eat a few now and then as we always did. Still it seemed as though the bucket would never fill up. At last we had enough and started back to the house.

As soon as we reached the clearing and could see the house, we knew we were in trouble.

"Oh, no!" Sarah Jane cried as we surveyed the scene before us.

Everyone seemed to be in motion. Roy was galloping toward the woods where we stood. Reuben was racing for the barn, carrying something that looked like a small pig in doll clothes, and Pep was running between the two

of them, not sure whom to follow. The only still figures were Mrs. Carter, who was lying on the porch steps, and ma, who was kneeling beside her, wiping her friend's face with a cloth.

"I think they've found the pig," Sarah Jane observed.

I nodded.

"We'd better get moving," Sarah Jane said. "We're in for it sooner or later!"

By this time, Roy had reached us, and he breathlessly reported the news. "Someone stole Mrs. Carter's baby and left a pig in the buggy. You're going to get it, because it's wearing your doll clothes."

"I told you Lucy would sleep for hours," Sarah Jane declared impatiently. "She didn't even cry to let them know where she was. How did we know they'd look for her before she woke up?"

I was sure that argument wasn't going to impress ma, because I had used similar logic on her before without success. But the sooner they found out where the baby was, the better off we would be.

Once everyone stopped long enough to listen, Sarah Jane and I explained everything, and Mrs. Carter was reunited with her baby. When she saw that Lucy was safe, she told ma not to punish us.

"They just didn't think. I know they didn't mean to be bad."

"They'd better learn to think," ma replied crossly.

"Do you suppose you can ring the dinner bell without doing something foolish?" she said to me.

Soon pa came in from the field and washed for dinner. Sarah Jane and I sat as quietly as we could, hoping that no one would pay any attention to us and praying that the boys wouldn't tell pa what had happened.

Unfortunately they didn't need to. Pa sat down, asked the blessing, and looked around the table. "Would someone tell me what the fool pig is doing down in the pen with doll rags on? The sow won't even let it come near her." Pa waited for someone to reply.

Sarah Jane and I avoided his glance, Roy sputtered into his glass, and Reuben looked disgusted. Then, to our surprise, ma and Mrs. Carter began to laugh!

Pa laughed too, when he heard the story, making Sarah Jane and I feel better. . . ."

Grandma picked up the pan of beans and went to check on her bread. I sat on the steps and looked out over the front yard. I could almost see the buggy and that funny pig!

4

When Grandma Needed Prayer

"GRANDMA," I SAID, "I've lost the book that is due at the library tomorrow. Have you seen it?"

"No, I haven't. Did you look all over your room?"

"I've looked everywhere!" I said. "It just isn't here. I'll have to pay for it if I don't find it, and I haven't any money. What shall I do?"

"We could pray about it," grandma said. "We'll ask the Lord to help us find it."

"I didn't know the Lord cared about library books. I thought we were just supposed to ask for big stuff."

"Nothing is too small for God to care about when it involves one of his children," grandma replied.

We prayed about the lost book, and I went to get ready for bed. When I turned back the covers, my book was under the pillow!

"Look, grandma," I called. "Here it is! That was a quick answer to prayer, wasn't it?"

Grandma came to my door and nodded her head. "I'm not surprised. The Lord says 'Before you call, I will answer.' He knows just what we need all the time."

"We didn't really have to pray then. The book was here anyway, and the Lord knew I needed it."

"Get into bed," grandma said, "and I'll tell you why we should always pray, even though God knows our needs. . . ."

When I was a little girl, we always had family prayer in our home, and pa expected each of us to pray. We were brought up to believe that God always hears and answers when his children call.

But I was often a very stubborn child. There were times when I didn't want to do what I knew was right. The morning that I remember was one of those times. Pa had promised that the whole family could go with him to a cattle auction in the next county.

"There is a homemaking exhibit for the ladies, I hear," he said to ma. "You will enjoy that."

"Even me?" I asked excitedly. "I can go too, pa?"

"Pa said it was for *ladies!*" Roy put in. "That sure wouldn't include you."

I started to protest, but ma interrupted. "Now, Roy, don't start something you'll be sorry for. Of course that includes you, Mabel. Have we ever left you at home?"

I was excited, and I could hardly wait for the day to come. It finally did, and we were up before daybreak to have breakfast and get started. I was in such a hurry to leave that I didn't want to finish the meal.

"You'll wish you had before you see dinner time," ma warned. "You'd better eat."

Ma didn't know how true that would be.

After breakfast, pa reached for the Bible.

"Oh, pa!" I protested. "We aren't going to take time for prayer this morning, are we? Couldn't we do it when we get home tonight? It's a long way to the exhibition grounds!"

Pa looked at me with surprise. "God always comes first in this house, you know that, Mabel. We want to start our day by talking to him."

"Well, *I* don't," I replied crossly.

It's a wonder ma didn't spank me right then. But she didn't. She just looked at me quietly. "All right, Mabel, you won't need to pray this morning."

Somehow the day didn't seem quite as exciting to me now. I knew I had been horrid and should have been punished.

We got into the buggy and started out. I sat very quietly while the boys chattered about what they would see and do. As the sun came up, and we neared the grounds, my spirits rose, and I began to think of the fun I would have.

"The first thing I want to do is find Sarah Jane. We want to look at everything that is here."

"You won't have far to look," ma replied. "I see her standing by the buggies, waiting for you."

Sarah Jane was hopping from one foot to the other with excitement. "Hurry, Mabel," she called. "I've been waiting and waiting for you. What took you so long?"

I started to say something about having prayer before we left, but then thought better of it. "We're here now," I said. "Let's go."

We ran off toward the big tent that held the homemaking exhibit, and our mothers followed close behind.

"Oh!" Sarah Jane exclaimed, "we'll never

see all this! I didn't know there were that many quilts in the whole world! Have you ever seen so many things?"

"No," ma laughed. "I guess I haven't. And look at all the baked goods and canned food! We'd better get started, or we'll miss something."

For a long time Sarah Jane and I trailed along after our mothers, looking at the displays and pointing out what we liked best. Shortly before noon, the ladies sat down to rest.

"Don't you girls wander off too far," ma said to us. "We'll be eating in just a little while."

"May we go outside and look around, ma?" I asked.

"I guess that would be all right. But don't get out of sight of the tents, will you?"

"Oh, no," we promised. "We'll stay right close by."

And we fully intended to do that. There were a number of tents with different displays in them, and we were going to look at those and come right back. A large woods lay at the end of the exhibit grounds, and as we approached the edge of it, Sarah Jane stopped and grabbed my hand.

"Look, Mabel. Do you see that?" She pointed toward the big trees.

"What is it? Did one of the calves get away

from the animal tent already?"

Sarah Jane shook her head. "I don't think so. It looks like a fawn to me. Let's go see."

Quietly we tiptoed to the end of the clearing and approached the tree. It was a fawn, and it was watching us.

"He doesn't seem to be afraid," I said. "He's not running away."

Slowly we walked toward the little animal, hoping that we could pet it. As we came closer, he turned and started into the woods. If he had run, we would have given up and gone back. But he walked slowly and let us keep him in sight.

"Isn't he pretty?" Sarah Jane exclaimed. "I wish he'd stop and let us get closer. If we hurry any faster, I'm afraid we'll scare him."

So without thinking that we were in a strange woods, we followed the fawn for a long time. Finally he disappeared from view, and we turned to go back to the exhibit grounds.

"We've come a long way, Sarah Jane. I can't see the edge of the woods from here. What if we go in the wrong direction?"

"You can't go in the wrong direction if you just turn around from the way you've been going," she said. And to prove it, she turned around and started back. I followed, assured that she knew how to get to the exhibit ground.

Even though the sun was overhead by now, it was cool and shady in the woods. We walked on for what seemed like a long time; then Sarah Jane stopped.

"We don't seem to be going anyplace," she said. "I don't think we walked this far."

"You mean you don't know the way back? You acted like you did. How come we've gone the wrong way if all we had to do was turn around?"

"I guess we didn't turn around far enough," Sarah Jane admitted. "We'd better stop and think about it a minute."

We stopped and sat down on a log. The woods didn't seem as friendly anymore, and I began to feel anxious. Sarah Jane looked around thoughtfully. "My brother says that moss always grows on the north side of trees."

"What has that got to do with anything?" I asked crossly. "We don't even know what direction we came from. We could stand in the woods with our noses pointed north all day and never get out."

"You don't have to be cross," Sarah Jane said. "I was trying to think of something to help us. What do you think we should do?"

"I'm sorry," I said, "but I'm getting sort of worried. Besides, I'm awfully hungry. It must be way past dinner time by now. Do you suppose they'll go ahead and eat without us?"

"Probably," Sarah Jane replied glumly. "They won't know we went away from the grounds. We were sure dumb to follow that fawn."

We sat for a few more minutes, staring into the woods, then got up and started to walk again. Everything looked alike, and it seemed as though we had seen every tree in the woods.

"Look," said Sarah Jane in disgust. "This is the same log we were just sitting on. We've just gone around in circles. I think we'd better stop and pray about it. The Lord can help us find the way back."

Suddenly I remembered that I had stubbornly refused to pray that morning. Now that I needed help, I was ashamed to ask God for it. I was sorry that I had been so rebellious and foolish.

"You pray," I said to Sarah Jane as we sat back down on the log.

"Dear Lord, please send someone to find us," she prayed. "Or show us the way back to our folks. Thank you.

"Now what shall we do?" she asked.

"Pa told us that if we ever got lost in our woods we should sit still until someone finds us. Maybe we better do that in this woods, too."

"I guess so. We didn't do much good moving around, so we'd better stay right here and let

God send someone after us."

"I hope he doesn't send Roy." I sighed. "He'd never let us forget it. Do you suppose we better add to the prayer that we'd rather have pa come?"

"I'm so hungry I don't care who he sends," Sarah Jane whined. "Anyone would look good to me right now."

It seemed like we sat on that log for hours. We sang all the songs we knew, and recited all the poems we had learned. As the shadows lengthened in the woods, it became harder to sit still, rather than trying to find our way out.

"Do you suppose we better remind God that we're still here?" Sarah Jane asked.

"I don't think we need to. I'm sure he's already told our folks where we are."

"I wish they would hurry up and come then," Sarah Jane said. "It must be almost night."

Finally both of us fell asleep. The next thing we knew we were being picked up in strong arms and carried toward the exhibit grounds.

"I knew you'd come," I said to pa. "We asked the Lord to send someone. Did he tell you where to find us?"

"Yes, I'm sure he did," pa replied. "And I'm glad you remembered to stay in one place."

"Pa," I said, "I'm sorry I didn't pray this morning. I won't ever do that again."

Pa hugged me, and I knew he had forgiven me. Soon we were back with our families. Were we surprised to find out that we had only been gone for about two hours!

"Girls!" Roy said in disgust. "They don't even know which way is which!"

"We do so!" I retorted. "It's just that the trees all look alike, and this is a strange woods."

"I'm glad the Lord was watching over you girls," ma said. "If he doesn't, there's not much hope for either one of you, I'm afraid."

We ate dinner, and spent the rest of the day close to ma. Even though the Lord knew where we were, I was certainly glad we could pray that day!

5

The Stranger

GRANDMA TAPPED on the kitchen window to signal that my lunch was ready.

"Who was your little friend?" she asked as I came into the kitchen. "I saw you swinging with someone."

"I don't know," I replied. "He followed me up the lane when I came from the mailbox, and we just started playing."

"You know his name, don't you?"

"No, I didn't ask him."

Grandma looked surprised. "You played together all morning and didn't ask his name?"

I shrugged. "I didn't have to call him for

anything. He was right there. He didn't ask me my name, either."

Grandma laughed and put the soup and homemade bread on the table. "I guess you're right. Names aren't as important as some other things you can know about a person. In fact, I can remember that our whole family did something like that once."

"You did? Tell me about it."

"It was right here on this farm," grandma began, "although this kitchen looked a lot different then. There was no electricity or running water, you know, and ma had just the wood stove to cook on. . . .

Early one fall, ma and I went to the woods to gather nuts. It was a beautiful day, and we took our time getting back. When we got in sight of the house, ma stopped and pointed toward the porch.

"Look, Mabel," she said. "There's someone sitting on the porch. Now who could that be?"

There was no buggy in the yard, nor was there a horse in sight.

"Whoever it is must have walked," I said. "Unless someone brought him and went away again."

By this time we could see that a rather elderly man was seated in pa's chair, with an old black satchel beside him. His coat was folded over his knees, and he seemed quite comfortable.

"Who is he, ma? I can't remember seeing him before."

"Neither do I," ma said. "He must have come to see your pa about something. Dear me, I wonder how long he's been sitting there?"

We hurried across the yard. As we neared the porch, the old man stood up and smiled.

"I'm sorry we weren't here when you came," ma said. "Have you been waiting long?"

"Oh, no," he replied. "Just a few minutes. It's nice here in the sun. Been pretty frosty these nights, hasn't it?"

"Yes, it has," ma agreed. "Really fine weather for gathering nuts. Won't you come in, Mr. . . .?"

"Thank you, ma'am. Yes, I will." He picked up his satchel and held the screen door open for us. Ma put the baskets on the table, and the man sat down by the fireplace.

"If you'll be good enough to bring me your ma's iron and a hammer, Missy," he said to me, "I'd be pleased to shell those nuts for you."

Ma looked startled. "Oh, you don't need to work. I'm sure pa will be in very soon."

"I don't mind a bit," our visitor declared. "It would be a pleasure."

So I brought the old black iron that ma had heated on the wood stove, and the man sat and cracked the nuts we had gathered. From time to time, ma glanced at him with a puzzled look on her face. He had said nothing to indicate what his business was, but we presumed that pa would know.

As we worked around the kitchen getting ready for supper, the old man talked about the weather, the beauty of the woods behind the house, and the extraordinary quality of the nuts this year.

After a while, I followed ma into the pantry. "Shall I ask him his name, ma?" I whispered.

"I should say not!" ma replied. "That wouldn't be polite. Pa will be in any minute now. He will tell us who that man is soon enough."

As it happened, ma was in the cellar when pa and the boys finally came in from the barn. The old gentleman stood up and held out his hand.

"Howdy, sir," he said. "This sure has been a beautiful day to work in the fields, hasn't it?"

"Yes," pa agreed. "It has been a good day."

Reuben and Roy stared at the man until pa nudged them forward. "Shake hands, boys," he said, "then get washed for supper."

By the time ma returned from the cellar, pa and the visitor were discussing the crops and the possibility of a hard winter.

"The Lord has been good to you to give you two fine sons to help you here," the old man said.

"Yes," pa agreed, "he has blessed us. We have a good farm and a comfortable home. The Lord has promised that his children should lack for nothing, and we haven't. We thank him for that."

"And missy, too. I daresay she's a big help to her ma. You go to school, do you?" the stranger asked me.

"Yes, sir. I can read almost as well as the boys can."

"That's what you . . ." Roy started to say, but Reuben kicked his foot under the table, and he didn't finish.

"Can you now?" the man said. "I just happen to have a book in my satchel that you could read to us. How would you like that?"

That suited me just fine. I loved to read, and we didn't have many books come our way. As soon as the dishes were cleared away, we all sat around the fireplace. Pa led us in our evening prayers, and our visitor joined in, asking God's blessing on this fine family.

The boys were not anxious to hear me read, but curiosity kept them there as the visitor opened his bag and felt around inside.

"Ah! Here it is." He pulled out a slender,

leather-bound volume and handed it to me. Ma took up her sewing, and pa and the boys sat back to listen. I opened the book and began to read. "Poems by Henry Wadsworth Longfellow."

I turned the page eagerly. "Under a spreading chestnut tree/ The village smithy stands. . . ."

Long before it seemed possible, the fire began to die down, and the lamp flickered.

"Why! Would you look at what time it is!" ma exclaimed. "You children must get to bed."

"Oh, can't we finish the book, ma?" I begged. "It won't take too much longer, and I like these poems."

The boys agreed and pleaded to stay up longer.

"Not tonight," pa said firmly. "We all need to be getting our sleep. Tomorrow is another day."

Reluctantly, the boys headed for the upstairs, and I went to my room.

"I sure do thank you for your hospitality," the man said to pa. "It was mighty nice of you to have me. I hope it's no bother."

"No bother at all," pa boomed. "You're welcome, I'm sure. Now you just take your satchel into the back room."

Pa escorted the old man to his room, then returned to the living room where ma was banking the fire for the night.

"Really, pa," she said. "I think you might have told us what his name was."

Pa stopped still in the middle of the room and looked at ma in amazement. "You mean you don't know who that man is?"

"Why, no," ma said. "I thought he came to see you."

"I never saw him until this afternoon," pa declared. "I supposed he was someone the preacher had sent to spend the night."

Pa sat down at the table and stared at ma. "Didn't he say anything at all about where he's from or how he happened to be here?"

Ma shook her head. "He acted as if he knew us, and we were expecting him. I don't think he ever did call us by name, though."

"Well, can you beat that," pa said. "I never heard of such a thing. What do we do now?"

They agreed that it would not do to knock on his bedroom door and say, "Who are you?" Neither could they ask where he came from and how long he was staying, since presumably they should already have known that. Finally they agreed to wait until morning and see if there would be a clue to the stranger's identity.

"Perhaps he is the 'angel unaware' that the Bible speaks of," pa said. "We certainly have had a pleasant evening."

The next morning, I came into the kitchen just as Reuben returned from the barn.

"What are you doing back so soon?" ma asked him.

"Pa didn't need me," Reuben replied. "The visitor has the milking almost done. He told pa he has to leave right after breakfast. Who is he, anyway, ma?"

"I wish I knew." Ma sighed. "I don't even know how I can find out without being rude."

"I'd just ask him," I declared. "I'd just say, 'What's your name?' "

"I'm sure you would," ma said. "But that's hardly the polite thing to do. You'd better turn your talents to setting the table for breakfast."

During the meal, the stranger spoke of the fine evening we had spent together and thanked us for sharing our home with him. As he rose to leave, he reached into his pocket, took out the small book we had been reading, and handed it to me.

"Here, missy," he said. "I want you to have this as a remembrance. It was a pleasure to hear you read it."

We stood on the porch and watched the old man as he trudged down the lane. At the gate, he turned and waved at us.

"Well," ma said, "we don't know anymore now than we ever did."

"Maybe he put his name in the book," Reuben suggested.

I looked, and found that the stranger had written, "From a friend. October, 1880."

That was all. . . ."

"Didn't you ever find out who he was?" I asked. "He wasn't a tramp, was he?"

"No." Grandma laughed. "He wasn't a tramp. Pa did find out about him later. He was an uncle of our neighbor Ed Hobbs, and was on his way to the southern part of the state. Mr. Hobbs had told him that he was sure the O-'Dells would welcome him for a night. Mrs. Hobbs was to let ma know he was coming, but somehow everyone thought somebody else had taken care of it, and nobody had. That never could happen in the city, because we're more careful about strangers."

Grandma began to clear the table. "We miss a lot by not being able to trust everyone like we did back then."

6

The Big Snow Storm

I PRESSED MY NOSE against the kitchen window to watch the snow fall in big flakes past the glass.

"Do you think we will be snowed in, grandma?" I asked.

Grandma came over and looked out the window. "Probably not. If the wind comes up tonight the snow may drift around the house, but it isn't deep enough to keep us snowbound. It doesn't seem to snow as much as it did when I was a little girl. I can remember walking on frozen snow as high as the fence tops."

"Really? I never saw that much snow. That

must have been lots of fun!"

"It was, as long as you didn't hit a soft spot and fall in. Then you could be in snow over your head, and you'd need help to climb out."

"I wish it would do that again," I said. "I can't think of anything more fun than being snowed in."

"Well, I can think of a few things more fun," grandma replied, "but there probably isn't anything much more exciting. There are a lot of things to take care of on a farm if you know you can't get out for a while. I remember one snow storm when things almost got out of hand around here. . . .

It was in the early spring, and the ground had been clear for several weeks. We thought that winter was over, and it would soon be warm. One morning when it was still dark pa came in from the barn.

"Boys," he said to Reuben and Roy, "I'll need your help after breakfast to get extra feed down for the animals. I smell a storm in the air."

"What does a storm smell like, pa?" I asked him.

Pa looked puzzled. "I guess I can't tell you that. It's something you just know when you've lived in the country all your life."

"I've lived in the country all my life," I replied, "and I don't remember ever smelling a storm."

Roy looked at me in disgust. "What do you know about anything? You probably wouldn't know a storm if you got caught in it."

"I would so," I retorted. "I'm as smart as you are!"

"Enough," pa said. "We've heard all this before. Let's eat and get to work."

After breakfast, pa and the boys departed for the barn, and ma and I started to clean up the kitchen. As it began to get light, I looked out the window. This day looked as nice as the ones before it.

"Pa must have smelled wrong," I said. "It's too nice to storm."

"He may have," ma laughed, "but I wouldn't count on it. He's a pretty good weatherman."

As the morning wore on, it began to look as though pa was going to be right. Clouds came in, and by dinner time it was almost as dark as evening.

"We'll get extra wood after dinner," pa announced. "And it might be well to bring the rope from the barn."

I knew what that was for. Pa had a long, heavy rope that he tied to the barn door and stretched along the path to the kitchen door. In a heavy blizzard it was sometimes hard to see the barn from the house, and the rope was a guide to go out and feed the animals.

Before dinner was over, it had begun to snow hard. When they finished eating, pa and the boys went back out. Ma hurriedly cleared the table, then put on her heavy sweater.

"I'm going to the cellar, Mabel," she said. "I think I'd better bring up some canned goods and vegetables before the snow covers the doors. Would you mind starting the dishes? I'll help as soon as I get back."

Ma took a large basket with her and opened the back door. Immediately it was pulled out of her hands and banged against the house.

"Mercy! Come and close the door, please, Mabel. This is turning into a real blizzard."

And indeed it was. After ma left, I stood at the window and watched her struggle to get the cellar door open. She finally managed to get one side up, and apparently deciding that was enough, she disappeared into the cellar. I watched the storm for a few minutes, then reluctantly started the dishes.

Sometime later pa came around the corner of the house, and seeing the cellar door open, muttered something about those careless boys, and closed the door. When he brought a load of wood into the kitchen, he stopped to warm his hands over the stove.

"Where's ma?" he asked me.

"She went to get some vegetables. She said she'd be right back to help me with the dishes."

Pa nodded and went out again. He and the boys brought in load after load of wood; then they began to carry in water. Pa stopped again by the stove.

"What's the matter here? The fire is dying down. Where's ma?"

"I told you, pa," I answered. "She went to get some vegetables. She sure has been gone a long time. I've had to do all these dishes alone."

Suddenly pa looked horrified. "Vegetables! You mean ma went to the cellar for vegetables? Why didn't you say so?"

He dashed out the door and down the stairs to the cellar, leaving me saying "I thought you knew!" to an empty kitchen.

In a moment they were back, with pa carrying the basket, and ma rubbing her hands together and stamping the snow from her feet.

"That cellar is not the warmest place on the farm," she said. "I'd rather have been shut in the barn if you were going to leave me locked up all afternoon. I'll probably catch my death of foolishness."

And sure enough, by evening ma was feverish and beginning to cough.

"I'm sorry, Maryanne," pa said anxiously.

"That was a terrible thing for me to do. I was in such a hurry I just didn't think."

"Don't worry about it," ma said hoarsely. "It'll probably be just a slight cold. I'll get to bed early, and it will be all better by morning."

Unfortunately, ma was wrong. By morning her cold, and the storm, had worsened. When she decided to stay in bed, I realized that she was sicker than I had ever known her to be.

Pa and the boys were glad to have the rope when they went to milk and feed the animals, but they knew there was no chance of getting farther than the barn.

"As soon as the storm lets up, I'll go and get the doctor for ma," pa told us. "I guess you'll all have to help me keep things going until she's well."

Since everyone had to stay in the house, pa didn't worry about the outside. His biggest problem seemed to be getting the meals.

"This always looks easy when ma does it," he said to me the next morning. "Ask her how many cups of baking powder to put in the pancakes."

"Cups!" ma croaked when I asked her. "Mercy on us! He'll kill us all with indigestion! Tell him two tablespoons to three cups of flour."

I was kept busy running between the

kitchen and the bedroom for instructions. Finally, ma suggested that he stick to things like meat and potatoes and other vegetables that didn't require mixing. "I'll be up right away to make bread," she said. "I don't think you'll run out before tomorrow."

We didn't run out of bread, but ma was not up the next day. Pa was worried. He stood at the window and watched the snow swirl around the porch. The barn was not visible from the house.

"I don't know how we'll get the doctor if this doesn't stop," he said. "We'll have to ask the Lord to take care of ma until the storm is over."

"We could ask him to tell the doctor to come," I suggested. "Then you wouldn't have to go after him."

"Yes," pa said. "We could do that all right. God could certainly send the doctor here if that's his will."

That night, just as we were ready to go to bed, we were startled by a loud banging on the door. When pa opened it, there, surrounded by snow and wind, stood the doctor!

"Thank the Lord!" pa said as he pulled him into the kitchen. "We prayed that you would come!"

"What do you mean you prayed that I would come?" the doctor exclaimed. "You didn't even

61

call for me! I was trying to get home from the Gibbs's place, and I was beginning to think I wouldn't make it anywhere when I saw your light."

"Anyway," pa said, "the Lord sent you, and we're grateful."

The doctor took care of ma and stayed until the following day. When the wind stopped blowing, the men and the boys were able to dig through the drifts. Soon everything was back to normal. That was certainly some storm; probably the worst I can remember. . . ."

"After that, I guess you believed your pa could smell a storm, didn't you?" I asked.

"Yes." Grandma laughed. "We didn't doubt him again. But I lived many more years in the country, and I don't think I was ever good at sniffing out the weather."

I returned to the window to watch the snow and wish I could be snowbound, just once.

7

Grandma and the Slate

THE YEAR I WAS in the second grade, I stayed with grandma in her old home on the farm for several months.

"We will have to get you in school next week," grandma said. "We'll go into town and talk to the principal tomorrow."

I was disappointed. "I thought maybe I wouldn't have to go to school since we'll only be here until Christmas. Couldn't you teach me at home? You were a school teacher once."

Grandma laughed. "The state doesn't think much of children not being in school. You wouldn't want the truant officers coming to ask about you, would you?"

I agreed that I wouldn't. Suddenly a new idea occurred to me. "Will I go to school in the same place you did, grandma? I'd really like that!"

"I'm afraid not. You won't even go to the school your mother attended. There's a big new school in town now. I think you'll like it."

I wasn't at all sure about that, but I knew that as soon as summer ended, I would be in school. I went out in the yard to swing on the old tire Uncle Roy had fixed for me and tried to forget about the future.

A little while later, grandma called me. "Come here and see what I've found. I thought this might be in the attic. You won't use it in school as I did, but you might like to play with it here at home."

The object she held in her hand was about nine inches wide and twelve inches long. It had a wooden frame around it and looked like a piece of blackboard.

"What is it, grandma?" I asked.

"It's a slate," grandma replied. "This is what we used to write our lessons on. We would do our arithmetic problems on here, then when the teacher had checked them, we rubbed them off and wrote our spelling words or writing lesson. It never wore out or had to be thrown away like paper does. A slate was as important to us as our books."

I took the slate and turned it over. There at the top were the letters of the alphabet and the numbers from *O* through *9*. Underneath them was a short poem:

> God made the little birds to sing,
> And flit from tree to tree;
> 'Tis He who sends them in the spring
> To sing for you and me.

"This was really yours?" I asked. "Where is the chalk and eraser to go with it?"

Grandma laughed. "We didn't have chalk then. We used a slate pencil to write with, and we brought an old piece of flannel from home to clean it off. I'm afraid the pencil has been lost long ago, but chalk works very well on it. I'm sure we have some of that around."

Grandma found a piece of chalk, and I sat down to copy the little poem on the slate. Just as I had finished and was going to show grandma, Uncle Roy came into the kitchen where I sat. He stopped at the table and looked at the slate.

"Well, well," he said. "If that isn't my old slate! Wherever did your grandma find it?"

"Your slate," I said in surprise. "Grandma said it was her slate."

Uncle Roy chuckled. "She's right, too. Did

she tell you how she managed to get it?"

Grandma came into the kitchen. "No, I didn't. Are you sure you want me to tell her that?"

Uncle Roy's eyes twinkled, and he replied, "Guess you'll have to now. I already told her it was mine. I'll just listen to be sure you have the story straight."

He sat down at the table with a cup of coffee and a cookie, and grandma began. . . .

Roy is right. The slate did belong to him, and he was very proud of it. As I remember, it was ordered from the catalog when Roy started school. He was two years ahead of me, but I couldn't see any reason why he should have a nice slate like that if I couldn't. Ma tried to explain that I would have one of my own when I started school, but naturally that was longer than I wanted to wait. Roy knew how eager I was to use that slate, and he liked to tease me about it.

"You're too young to have a slate, Mabel," he would say. "You'd probably break the pencil. Anyway, you can't write yet."

"I can try," I would say. "And I'll be careful. I won't hurt it a bit."

But Roy kept his slate out of my reach in spite of all my pleading. One evening after supper, the boys were doing their lessons at the kitchen table when pa looked up from his reading.

"Roy, did you put the goat in the barn as I asked you to?"

"Oh, no, pa. I forgot. I'll do it as soon as I finish my lessons."

"Be sure you do," pa said. "It's going to be cold tonight. She shouldn't be left out."

Pa went into the other room to read to ma as she sewed, and Roy looked over at me where I sat by the stove playing with my doll.

"Say, Mabel. How would you like to write on my slate?"

I dropped the doll and came over to the table. "Could I, Roy? Could I?"

"Sure you can. If you go out and put the goat in the barn."

Roy knew that I would not so much as step onto the back porch after dark, let alone go clear out to the barn. I shook my head. "Pa told you to go."

"I know, but I'm busy. There's nothing out there to get you."

I continued to shake my head. Finally, Roy said, "What if I give you the slate?"

"Give it to me? Really give it to me all for myself?"

"That's right. It's all yours if you go out and put the goat in the barn."

I considered this carefully. I wanted that slate more than anything. On the other hand, there was a lot of blackness between the house and the barn. Did I dare do it?

"Will you leave the kitchen door open?" I asked fearfully.

"Sure," Roy replied. "Why, I'll even put a lantern on the steps. It won't take you but a minute."

If ma or pa had been in the room, he would never have suggested such a thing. But he did love to tease me.

Somehow I found enough courage to race out to the barn, shove the goat inside, and race back. Breathlessly I dropped into my rocking chair. When I could speak again, I reminded Roy of his promise.

"Oh," he said. "I told you I'd give you the slate, but I meant when you were old enough to go to school. You're too little to use it now."

I looked at him in disbelief. As the enormity of what he had done began to sink in, I opened my mouth and howled. I cried louder than I ever had before, or since, I guess. The noise brought ma running from the other room.

"What in the world is going on here? Mabel, are you hurt? What happened?"

I was crying too hard to answer. Big tears were running down my face and onto my dress. Roy was too astonished at the turn of events to be able to explain, so Reuben told ma what had happened. When he finished, ma took me in her lap and smoothed my hair back.

"Don't cry, Mabel. There's nothing to cry about. The slate is yours right now."

"Right now!" Roy yelped. "I have to have it for school. She can't have it right now!"

"I think she can," ma replied quietly. "We'll find an old piece of slate for you to use. Give it to her, please."

Reluctantly, Roy handed over the slate. He certainly hadn't intended the joke to go this far. I clutched it to me and ran out to show pa. Roy went back to his lessons, a smarter boy than he had been a few minutes earlier. . . .

"Isn't that how it happened?" grandma said to Uncle Roy.

"It certainly was," he replied. "I carried an old broken piece of slate to school all the rest of that year. I should have learned my lesson about teasing right then, shouldn't I?"

"Yes," grandma laughed. "But you didn't."

Grandma turned to me. "Just watch out he doesn't get that slate away from you."

"Oh, I wouldn't do that," Uncle Roy replied. "But while I'm working I'll think of some tricks your grandma pulled that were as bad. Then it will be my turn to tell a story."

8

A Pig in a Poke

"YOUR SURPRISE PACKAGE came in the mail this morning," grandma said to me as I came home for lunch.

"Oh, goody! Where is it?" I asked.

"Here on the table. Now don't be too disappointed if it isn't all you thought it would be."

I had ordered a "mystery box" from a magazine ad, imagining all sorts of lovely things that might be inside.

"I guess you had twenty-five cents worth of pleasure waiting for it," grandma said when she saw the flimsy little toy the box contained.

"Next time I'll just spend my quarter at the

store where I can see what I'm getting," I said. "I wouldn't have paid a nickel for this."

"That's what's called, 'buying a pig in a poke.' You aren't the first one to do that."

"A pig in a poke! What does that mean?"

"A *poke* is an old word that means a 'sack,' " grandma replied. "If you buy a pig in a poke, you pay for it without looking at it first; then you have to take what you get. It's not the smartest way to do business, but you may learn a lesson from it."

"Have you ever bought a pig in a poke, grandma?"

"No, I didn't, but my brothers did. One of our neighbors sold his farm and was ready to move to another state. The day before he left, the boys went over to say good-bye. . . .

That night at the supper table, Reuben asked pa, "Could we use Nellie and the wagon in the morning? There's something we want to bring home from the Shaw's barn."

"What kind of something? We have several somethings in our own barn that could stand hauling off."

Reuben and Roy exchanged worried looks.

"Well," Reuben explained, "it's an old trunk. Mr. Shaw said we could have it, and whatever is in it, for just fifty cents."

71

"So, we put our money together and bought it," Roy added.

Pa put his fork down and looked at the boys. "Fifty cents! You mean you paid for the thing and didn't even look inside to see what you were getting?"

Reuben looked embarrassed. "We tried to," he mumbled, "but we couldn't get it open. Mr. Shaw said it hadn't been opened for fifty years or more, because no one could find the key."

"What in the world do you plan to do with a trunk full of who-knows-what that you can't even get into?" pa asked. "Couldn't you think of a better way to spend your money?"

"It seemed like a good idea at the time," Reuben explained. "We thought we'd get it open some way, and it might be something really valuable."

"Very likely!" pa snorted. "A trunk that has been sitting in the barn for fifty years is bound to be a real prize!"

"Can we take the wagon, then?" Reuben asked.

"Yes," pa replied, "go ahead and take it. I hope for your sakes it's worth your time and effort."

The boys were sure it would be, and they spent the rest of the evening talking about the treasure they would have.

"If there's anything you like, we'll give it to

you," Roy said to ma. "There might even be a doll or something for Mabel."

"Thank you," ma said. "That's generous of you. I just hope there's something in there you'll like."

Ma and I were at the window when the wagon pulled up the next morning, and we ran out to the porch. The boys looked delighted with themselves as they jumped down.

"Come and look, ma," Roy called. "Can we bring it in the kitchen?"

"Mercy, no! You're not bringing fifty years of barn dirt into my kitchen. Put it up here on the porch."

"But what if it rains?" Roy said anxiously.

Ma eyed the rusty old hinges and scuffed-up leather. "One more good rain couldn't do anything but improve it."

So, groaning and puffing, the boys tugged it up the steps. It was about three feet long and a foot and a half high.

"If it's worth its weight in anything at all, you'll have a fortune," ma said. "Did you hear a rattle in there?"

"No," Reuben replied. "It didn't move. It feels like one solid piece of iron to me."

"Part of the floor came up when we moved it," Roy put in. "I think Mr. Shaw's pa built the barn around it."

"Well, you boys can figure how you're going

to get it open while you're working today. Pa wants you to come help with the fence right away."

"Yes, ma'am," Reuben answered. "We'll work on it after dinner."

The boys went out to the field, and ma and I went back to the kitchen.

"What do you think is in there, ma?" I asked.

"I wouldn't have any idea. Usually folks keep things like quilts, or old photographs, or books, that sort of thing in them. I can't imagine what could be that heavy. I guess we'll have to wait until the boys get it open."

The rest of the morning I hung around the porch and watched the trunk. One time ma called to me from the kitchen door. "Haven't you anything better to do than watch that piece of junk? You're not going to know one thing more than you do now until it's opened."

She pushed the door out with her foot and handed me a pan. "As long as you're sitting there, you can at least snap the beans for dinner. I know how you feel. I'm anxious to know what's in there, too."

The morning passed slowly, but finally pa and the boys came in from the field. Reuben stopped at the barn and picked up a crowbar.

"Come and eat dinner first, boys," ma said. "If I'm not mistaken, you'll need all the strength you can get to pry that open."

Ma wasn't mistaken. Try as they would, the boys were not able to open the trunk. Red-faced and breathless, they left to join pa in the field.

"Oh, dear, we're never going to see what's in there," I said.

"I'm sure we will," ma replied. "Pa will help them this evening. They'll find some way to open it."

I spent the afternoon dreaming about all the wonderful things the trunk might hold and hoping that some of them might come to me. When supper was over, pa and the boys tackled the job again. The lid was rusted shut, and there seemed to be no place to get the crowbar under it. Finally, after much whacking and pounding, it began to look as though it might move.

"Let's give it another try," pa said. They all leaned hard on the crowbar, and the lid cracked open. We crowded up close as Reuben pushed up the creaky top to reveal the contents.

"Nails?" he said.

Pa looked over Reuben's shoulder and nodded his head. "Nails!"

"Nails!" Roy yelped. "Is that whole trunk full of rusty old nails?"

It certainly looked that way. The nails were

pitted and red and stuck together with rust. Reuben pushed his hand in as far as it would go and reported more of the same near the bottom.

"Seems to me I remember Bert Shaw saying that his father was a blacksmith before he bought the farm," pa said. "This must be all that's left of the smithy. I don't know what you can do with them, boys. I don't think there's much call for rusty nails."

"That was an awful lot of work for something as useless as this," Reuben sighed.

"Besides, we lost fifty cents on it," Roy added.

"Seems to me there's something in the Bible about laying up treasures where moth and rust will corrupt," ma said. "Maybe this is a good example to remind us."

"I guess so," Reuben said. "But I'd just as soon someone else's fifty cents had paid for it."

"Let's haul the thing out to the barn. Maybe the peddler will buy them when he comes by again," pa suggested.

The boys brightened up a little at that thought, and the trunk was moved to the barn. I don't remember whether the peddler took it or not, but I'm sure the boys didn't buy anything sight unseen again."

9

Grandma's Day Off

"WOULD YOU SET the table for me, please?" grandma asked as she was getting dinner ready.

"I don't want to," I replied.

Grandma looked at me in surprise. "You what?"

"I don't want to," I said, a little less bravely this time.

"I don't believe I asked if you wanted to. I asked if you would."

While I placed the knives and forks around the table, I muttered, "Molly Stone never has to do anything she doesn't want to."

Grandma looked at me thoughtfully. "I'm not sure that's always true. Having 'stuff' to do makes you part of the family. You'd be unhappy if you never had to work."

I'd like to try it some time, I thought.

Grandma seemed to have read my mind, for suddenly she laughed. "I wanted to try that once. I thought I was expected to do entirely too much around home, and that if I didn't have all my chores to do, I'd be perfectly happy."

"Did your mother let you try it?"

"Yes, she did," grandma replied, "and I'll tell you how it turned out after dinner."

When we had finished the dishes, grandma sat down with her sewing, and I pulled my chair up beside her. . . .

It was in the summer, the summer I was nine years old. Ma was very busy taking care of the garden, canning the early vegetables, and cooking for the hired men pa had working on the farm. My job was to make the beds, help with the dishes, sweep the floors and dust, feed the chickens, and bring the cows in from the pasture in the evening.

Actually those chores didn't take a lot of time if I got right at them, but I grumbled and fussed until my work seemed to use up most of the day. One morning ma became impatient with my complaining.

"You seem to forget that you're not the only one in the family who has work to do," she reminded me. "Pa and the boys aren't out in the fields playing ball, you know. Where would you be if no one in the family did any work for you?"

"I'd probably get along fine," I replied grumpily. "I could take care of myself if I didn't have all these other jobs to do."

Ma eyed me carefully for a moment. "All right. We'll try it and see. You finish up your work for today, and beginning tomorrow morning, you may do whatever you like. The rest of us will take over your chores."

"Do you really mean it, ma?" I exclaimed. "I don't have to do anything except what I want to?"

"I mean it. But remember, no one will do anything for you, either. That will be your responsibility."

I couldn't believe my good fortune, to actually be free to spend my time in any way I chose. I began to plan all the things I would do in the glorious days ahead.

That night at supper, pa regarded me thoughtfully. "I hear you're going to be a lady of independence."

"What does that mean, pa?" I asked.

"It means that you are going to take care of yourself and be your own boss."

I nodded happily. "That's right. Ma said I could do whatever I want—and no chores to finish first!"

Roy opened his mouth to say something, but a look from pa stopped him.

The following morning I awakened to the sound of voices in the kitchen. For a moment I wondered why ma had not called me. Then I remembered—this was *my* day! I could sleep half the morning if I wanted to! Suddenly I didn't want to. The whole exciting day stretched before me, and I needed to get an early start.

I jumped out of bed and reached for my clothes. They were not there! The dress and apron I had taken off the night before lay on the floor where I had dropped them, but there were no clean things on the chair where ma always placed them. I started to call her to come and help me, then decided against it. I could certainly get my own clothes out.

I dressed as quickly as I could and ran to the kitchen. To my surprise, the table was cleared, and ma was doing the dishes.

"Where is my breakfast?" I asked.

Ma didn't turn around. "That's your responsibility. You go ahead and get what you want."

That slowed me down a little. I hadn't counted on having to fix my meals. I could see that the family had eaten pancakes and ham and eggs, but that was hard for me to fix, especially since the pancake batter seemed to be all gone. I finally managed to cut a piece of bread and put jam on it. The heavy milk pitcher was too much for me to handle. Milk spilled out on the table and floor.

"That's too bad," ma said. "You know where the mop and bucket are, don't you?"

"Aren't you going to help me?"

"Why, no. You can take care of yourself."

When I had cleaned up the mess as best I could, I sat down at the table. A piece of bread and jam and no one to eat with seemed a poor way to start the day.

"I sure don't like to eat alone," I muttered.

"I'm sorry," ma said. "But I thought since you had no chores today, you'd rather sleep in than get up when we did."

This reminder of the good times ahead brightened my outlook somewhat, so I finished quickly and hurried outside. The day was bright and beautiful, and I skipped happily across the yard. Immediately I was surrounded by chickens.

"Oh, bother! You'll just have to wait. Ma will feed you as soon as she has time."

It seemed to me that they watched reproachfully as I ran on toward the brook. *It won't hurt 'em to wait a few minutes,* I thought. *This is my day.*

For a while I was happy, picking flowers and wading in the brook. I made a daisy chain to hang around my neck, then lay on my stomach to see myself in the water.

After what seemed like a long time, I looked up at the sun and saw that it was still only the middle of the morning. Time didn't go so fast when there was no one to play with. I thought of ma doing the dishes alone and making all the beds, and began to feel a little bit guilty.

But after all, I thought, *she did say I could do what I wanted to.* And that's what I was doing.

That morning went slower than any I had ever known. I was determined not to miss the dinner bell, so when it seemed close to noon, I started back to the house. I wasn't late, but another surprise awaited me.

The table was set for dinner, but at my place there was nothing but bread crumbs and a knife with jam on it!

Ma turned and smiled at me. "Did you have a nice morning?"

"Yes, ma'am. But don't I get to eat with you this noon?"

"Oh my, yes," ma replied. "Just clear away your breakfast things and set your place."

I did so, but my ideas about freedom were beginning to change.

"Shall I help put the food on?" I asked.

Ma looked surprised. "No, thank you. Just sit down, and we'll be ready to eat in a few minutes."

I sat down at the table and watched ma dish up the food. Something was just not right about this arrangement, and it made me feel uneasy. But I decided not to let the boys know how disappointing it was. When they and pa came in for dinner, I attempted to look happier than I felt.

"Well," pa boomed as he sat down at the table. "Do we have a visitor here today?"

"I'm not a visitor, pa," I said. "I live here!"

"Of course. How could I forget that?"

"I'd like to forget it sometimes," Roy added. "I could get along real well without her for a while."

I looked at ma quickly, afraid that she might decide to send me away so Roy could try it out, but she was giving him a disapproving look, and he bowed his head for prayer. Pa prayed as usual for the Lord to bless the food and the hands that prepared it. It occurred to me that I hadn't helped, so the blessing was not for me.

"What are you planning to do with your afternoon?" pa asked as he began to eat.

"I don't know exactly . . . but I'll have fun," I added quickly.

After dinner I wandered out to the porch and sat on the edge, swinging my feet. The rattle of dishes reminded me that mine would probably not be done unless I took care of it. When ma finished and left the kitchen, I crept to the door to look. Sure enough, there was my cup and plate. The rest of the table was cleared.

That's not fair! I thought. *Ma did the boys' dishes. She could have done mine, too.*

"And you could have helped her!" a little voice inside me said. "She did the boys' dishes, because they are out in the field working."

As quietly as I could, I rinsed off my dishes and brushed the crumbs from the table. I felt ashamed that I was the only one in the family who hadn't done anything all day. Even our dog, Pep, had taken the cows to the field that morning. Slowly I walked to my room to think things over. The unmade bed and the clothes on the floor looked worse than they had when I left them.

I picked up my clothes and made the bed, then sat down on the edge and looked around the room. Why had I thought that having no chores to do would be so wonderful? How had I planned to spend the time?

I picked up a mail order catalog and flipped

over a few pages, then put it down. Emily sat in the chair watching me, her sober, shoe-button, doll eyes inviting me to play. But I didn't feel like it. The clock in the parlor struck. Only one hour had passed since dinner time!

I sighed and walked to the window. Ma was in the garden picking vegetables for supper. Maybe she would let me help her get them ready.

"Ma, I'm tired of being a lady of independence. Could I shell the peas for you?"

"Are you sure you want to? What about your day off?"

"I think I've had enough of it. I can't think of anything I want to do."

"You've found out something important today!" ma said. "It often happens that if you don't do anything, there's nothing you *want* to do. That's a pretty sad way to live."

I agreed with ma, and I didn't try that again. . . .

Grandma looked at me, and her eyes twinkled. "Do you think you'd like to try it?"

I shook my head. "I don't think so. I guess it's nicer to have something to do."

10

How the News Spread

THE TELEPHONE RANG in the old farm kitchen, and grandma went to answer it. "Yes, Mr. Jenkins. I'll be in to get it this morning. Thank you."

Then grandma turned to me. "Would you like to walk to the store with me? The material is here. We can begin a dress for you this afternoon."

Of course I was eager to go, and we started off down the shady lane to the road.

"Did you have a telephone when you were a little girl, grandma?"

"Mercy, no. We didn't have electricity, or

running water, or a lot of other things we enjoy now. But we didn't mind. I guess you don't miss things you've never had."

"I don't know how you got along without a telephone. How did you find out what everybody was doing? Or what if you needed someone to come and help you?"

Grandma laughed. "That was easy. If something important happened, a neighbor would ride over and tell us. Or if we needed help, pa would send one of the boys to the nearest farm. News got around fast even without a telephone. In fact, it sometimes got around before it happened!"

"How could it do that? You can't tell news before it happens!"

"Some people can," grandma replied. "And it causes trouble sometimes, too."

"Did you do that grandma?"

"Yes, I'm afraid I did. I certainly didn't mean to do anything wrong, but I did like to talk. My tongue got me into difficulty more than once."

We had arrived at the store, so I waited until grandma had paid for the material, and we were on the way home before I asked, "What did you tell that hadn't happened, grandma? Did you make it up?"

"No," grandma replied, "not really. I told what I had heard, but I didn't know the whole story. I'll tell you how it happened. . . .

One of the things we looked forward to every spring was the visit of the peddler. For as long as I could remember, it was always the same one every year. When we would see his wagon coming down the lane, we would run to meet him. If he came in the morning, he stayed for midday dinner. If he came in the afternoon, he stayed for supper. Sometimes he could even be persuaded to spend the night.

Oh, that peddler's cart was wonderful! I'll never forget the splendid things we had to look at when he let down the sides of his wagon. Ma and I wanted to see all the cloth and ribbons and thread he had to display. Of course, the boys and I looked longingly at all the toys and games that were there.

Pa was interested in the tools and in the big grindstone, a large wheel made of something like cement. It sat on a wooden standard, and when the peddler pumped it with his foot, it went around and sharpened metal things. Ma brought her knives and scissors to be sharpened; pa brought the scythe and other tools.

The peddler was a wonderful man. He could mend pots and pans, or put new soles on our shoes, or even paint a new silver backing on a mirror for ma.

The whole day the peddler was here became a holiday, especially mealtime when we learned the news of the county. He knew what was happening to people we very seldom saw. This particular evening as we sat at the table, ma questioned him about some of her friends.

"Did you stop at the Blakes'?" she asked.

"Yes, ma'am. I was there just last week. Everyone is well, I think. Old Uncle Tosh doesn't rightly remember things as well as he used to, though. He thought I was there to marry Harriet!"

"Harriet has been married for fifteen years!" ma laughed. "Where was Wesley when Uncle Tosh said that?"

"He'd gone to the barn. Harriet said that every time Wesley is out of sight, Uncle Tosh forgets all about him, and wants to know when Harriet is planning to get married!"

"I hope Uncle Tosh knew who Wesley was when he came back to the house," pa remarked.

"Yes," the peddler nodded. "Most of the time he does. But sometimes he doesn't even remember Harriet. It must be hard to get old and have your past get away from you."

Ma and pa nodded in agreement.

"How about Luke and Hannah Edwards?" pa asked. "Are they getting on well?"

"Oh, yes. I saw them just three days ago.

Ruth Edwards bought a cloth for a wedding dress."

I put my fork down and looked at the peddler with surprise. "Ruth Edwards! Sarah Jane didn't tell me that Caleb was getting married!"

Caleb was Sarah Jane's oldest brother, and she and I knew he was courting Ruth Edwards. We had talked it over often, and made so many plans about what we were going to do at the wedding, that I was surprised Sarah Jane had withheld that information from me.

"Maybe they just didn't want two nosy little girls to know all about it," ma said. "Did it ever occur to you that they may not have told Sarah Jane?"

"But Caleb is her brother! You always know what happens to your own brother!" I turned to Reuben. "You'd tell me if you were getting married, wouldn't you?"

Reuben looked disgusted. "More likely, *you'd* tell me. When has anyone ever kept a secret from you?"

"That's enough," pa interrupted. "Have you forgotten that we have a guest?"

"Sorry, pa," Reuben said.

The subject was changed, but I was determined to get to the bottom of the story as soon as I could see Sarah Jane.

The next morning when she came to play, I

hurried her down to the creek where we could talk undisturbed.

"You didn't tell me that Caleb was getting married!" I accused her.

Sarah Jane's eyes grew round, and her mouth dropped open. "Married! My brother Caleb?"

"Yes, your brother. How many other Calebs do you know?"

Sarah Jane shook her head in bewilderment. "He's not getting married. I heard him tell pa he wouldn't marry until he is twenty. And he's only nineteen now."

"Well then," I said smugly, "Ruth Edwards is going to marry someone else. The peddler told us that she bought the goods for her wedding dress!"

I was pleased to see that this was news to Sarah Jane. At least she hadn't kept anything from me.

"I don't think Ruth would keep company with Caleb if she was going to marry someone else," she said. "He just rode over to see her last evening. Are you sure that's what the peddler said?"

"Positive." I nodded. "I was sitting right there and heard it all. What should we do now?"

Neither of us thought that possibly this affair was none of our business. Or that we ought to keep out of it. Instead we began planning how to get the news out as soon as possible.

"I think we should have a party for them," I said.

"But we don't know what day it will be," Sarah Jane protested.

"That doesn't matter. You can have a party to announce the wedding. Who shall we invite?"

We immediately set to work and invited everyone we saw to a party at Sarah Jane's house the next Saturday night. Of course, we didn't think to say anything to either of our families. But word got back to ma.

"What's this I hear about a party? Do Sarah Jane's folks know anything about it?"

"I don't think so. But I suppose she'll tell them."

"I certainly hope so. What is the party for?"

"It's a wedding party for Caleb and Ruth," I said. "It will be a surprise."

"Yes, it will," pa agreed, "especially since they aren't getting married for another year, and haven't even set the date yet."

"Why is Ruth doing her sewing so soon?" I asked in surprise. "The peddler said she bought the goods for her wedding dress."

"The peddler said *a* dress, not *her* dress. Ruth made a wedding dress for her cousin," ma informed me, crossly.

"Oh, no!"

"You'll be saying more than 'Oh!' before you get this story straightened out, young lady," pa scolded. "How could you girls pass along a story you didn't know was true?"

"We thought it was true," I said. "What shall we do now?"

"I suggest you tell Sarah Jane's folks about it first, then start uninviting all those people. Maybe this will teach both of you to check your news before you begin spreading it around. It's a good thing it wasn't a story that could have hurt someone."

We learned from that experience. By the time we heard the last of that mistake, we were heartily sorry that we had been so quick to tell our news. . . .

Grandma laughed. "Just think how much more mischief we could have done if we'd had a telephone!"

11

Charlotte

"GRANDMA," I wailed, "look what happened to Virginia!" I held up my doll so grandma could see how her leg had come away from her body. "Can she be fixed?"

Grandma examined the doll carefully. "I should think so. I imagine your Uncle Roy can mend her. Ask him when he comes in."

I sat on the steps and waited for Uncle Roy to come from the barn. As soon as he appeared I rushed to meet him.

"Grandma says you can fix Virginia, Uncle Roy. Will you try, please?"

Uncle Roy sat down and looked at the dangling leg. "I think a new piece of wire will take care of that. I'll fix it for you right after dinner."

He turned the doll over and laughed. "They sure don't make dolls like they used to. I remember a doll baby your grandma had."

"Was it Emily?" I asked.

"Mercy," Uncle Roy replied, "I don't know what she called it. I remember that I called it a mess—and so did ma."

At the dinner table that night, I questioned grandma. "What doll did you have that your mother and Uncle Roy thought was a mess?"

Grandma thought for a moment. "You must mean Charlotte. I'd almost forgotten about her. How did you remember, Roy?"

"I was with you when you found it," Uncle Roy said. "I tried to discourage you from taking it home, but you wouldn't listen to me."

"That's right. You were there, weren't you? I wonder why ma ever let me into the house with it."

"Because you were spoiled," Uncle Roy said, and he winked at me.

"What was the matter with it?" I asked. "Why shouldn't you bring it into the house?"

"Well," Grandma said, "it *was* a mess. No one in the family had anything good to say about it. But I thought any doll was lovable."

"Where did you find it?" I asked.

Grandma got up to clear the table and began the story. . . .

It was a rainy spring day in my first year of school. Roy and I were walking home together through the woods. I was lagging behind, as usual, and Roy had stopped to tell me to hurry up. He didn't particularly like his little sister tagging along, but he was responsible for me, so he didn't dare let me out of his sight.

"Come on, Mabel," he said. "You can walk faster than that. I've got chores to do before I can play. Just because you never have to do anything. . . ."

"I do so!" I retorted. "I help ma set the table, and I dry the knives and forks."

Roy snorted and turned to walk on.

"Wait a minute, Roy. Look at this."

Reluctantly he came back to where I stood. "Well, what is it?"

I bent over to pick something out of the mud. It was a doll—soaked almost beyond recognition. The features were nearly gone, and the clothes were torn and dripping. But to my motherly eye, it was beautiful. I hugged it to me as Roy watched in disgust.

"Ugh!" he groaned. "Throw it back! That's awful! Wait until ma sees what you've gotten all over your front!"

I looked down and saw that I had ruined my dress; mud and water were soaking through my apron. I knew that ma would not be pleased about that, but I couldn't throw the doll back.

"I'll take it home and clean it up," I said. "See, I'll hold it way out here." I held the doll at arm's length and began to run for home.

"It's too late to hold it way out there," Roy called after me. "You're already a mess. If I were you, I'd chuck that thing in the nearest hole."

I ignored him and continued on my way. When I ran into the kitchen, ma was horrified.

"Oh, Mabel! What happened to you? Did you fall down? And what is *that?*"

"It's a doll, ma. I found it in the woods and brought it home to take care of it. It just needs to be washed a little."

"It needs to be buried," Roy said. "I told her to leave it there, but she wouldn't listen." He put his lunch pail on the table.

"Where is your lunch pail, Mabel?" ma asked. "Did you leave it at school again?"

"No, I had it when I left school. I must have laid it down on the road when I stopped to pick up the doll."

Ma sighed. "Go back and get her lunch pail, Roy. I don't have anything else she can carry her lunch in."

"Oh, ma! Why can't she go back for it? It's her pail!"

Ma looked at Roy. "I guess I can put her lunch in with yours. You'll have to eat with her tomorrow."

"I'll go. I'll go."

"And you," ma said to me, "take that filthy thing out and wash it in the trough. Then come back and change your clothes."

I knew then that ma would let me keep the doll, but I didn't know what a surprise was in store for us. I hurried outside and swished it around in the water until most of the mud was gone, then brought it back to the kitchen.

"She's awfully heavy, ma, but I couldn't get any more water out."

"Put it on the back of the stove to dry. And change your dress. You're a sight."

When Reuben came in with a load of wood, he poked a finger into the doll. "What's this?" he asked ma.

"It's Mabel's doll. She found it on the way home from school."

"What's it stuffed with—rocks?"

"It's waterlogged," ma replied. "It won't be that stiff when it dries out."

By the time pa came in for supper, the doll had begun to smell musty.

"Phew!" pa's face twisted in mock disgust. "What smells like an old burlap bag? I hope it's not what we're having for supper."

"Hardly," ma answered. "It's Mabel's doll. It will probably take all night to dry out."

Several more comments were made about that doll before I went to bed: Roy offered it a decent burial, and Reuben declared he wouldn't touch it with a stick. Pa thought he'd better sit on the porch after supper and air out, since he smelled like a burlap bag himself after sitting by the stove.

I didn't think any of them were very funny. "Ma, you won't let anyone touch my doll, will you?"

"No, of course not. You get on to bed now."

"I'm going to name her Charlotte. Don't you think that's a pretty name?"

"Lovely. Now go to bed."

Sometime later that evening, pa and the boys were sitting in the kitchen. Pa was reading and the boys were doing their homework. Ma came in and found Reuben staring strangely at the stove.

"Ma, something's the matter with that doll."

"Is it burning?" ma said as she ran over to the stove.

"No, but I think it's alive!"

Pa looked up from his book. "Thy learning is turning thee mad," he teased.

"He's crazy," Roy added.

Nevertheless they all stared at the doll. Suddenly an arm jerked up; then one of the legs kicked out. Ma jumped back from the stove.

"Mercy! What's going on?"

As they watched, the doll became more lively. The head bobbed, and the arms and legs flopped wildly.

"Throw it on the floor!" pa ordered.

"Jump on it!" Roy shouted.

Ma gingerly picked up the doll and dropped it on the table, where it continued to toss and turn in a most lifelike way.

"At least it's beginning to smell better," Reuben said. "It smells almost like popcorn!"

"It *is* popcorn!" ma exclaimed. "That's what it's stuffed with."

And sure enough, that's exactly what was in it. After the doll stopped jumping, ma ripped it open and dumped out the corn.

Pa looked at the mess distastefully. "That old rag isn't worth stuffing again, is it?"

"No," ma admitted, "it isn't. But I promised Mabel I wouldn't let anyone touch her doll, so I'll have to put something in it."

"Fill it with catnip," Reuben suggested. "Maybe the cat will drag it off and lose it."

"Naw," said Roy. "Put pepper in it. Then Mabel will be glad to get rid of it."

But ma was more sympathetic. "If this old

rag makes Mabel happy, then she can have it. I'll wash it up and fill it with rice."

And that's what she did. I played with Charlotte for a long while. . . .

Grandma looked at my doll, which Uncle Roy had mended as he listened to the story. "You're right. They don't make dolls like they used to."

12

The Slate Pencil

GRANDMA CALLED ME in from the yard. "Would you please go to the store for me? I'm ready to bake rolls, and there isn't enough yeast. Take a quarter from my little change purse."

I found grandma's purse and put the quarter in my pocket. As I ran down the lane toward the road, it occurred to me that climbing over the fence and crossing the field would save some time, so I did just that. I was soon in the little general store that served our farming community.

"Mr. Jenkins," I said, "grandma needs some yeast."

Mr. Jenkins set three cakes of yeast on the counter. His eyes twinkled, and he smiled at me. "And what do *you* need?"

I knew what he meant. I was always allowed to pick a penny candy when I came to the store with grandma. But grandma wasn't here, and she hadn't said anything about spending a penny.

"How much change do I have from a quarter?" I asked.

"Seven cents," Mr. Jenkins replied. "The yeast is six cents a cake."

I thought that over quickly. I would have a nickel and two pennies back. I was sure grandma wouldn't care if I spent one penny, and if she were here, she might even say I could have them both. The longer I gazed at the candy display, the more certain I became that I needed two pennies worth as a reward for coming to the store alone.

As Mr. Jenkins handed me the candy and the nickel, a twinge inside me said this was not a really honest thing to do. That wasn't my money, and I hadn't asked if I might spend it. Nevertheless, I put the nickel in my pocket and started home. This time I took the long way around by the road.

"Thank you," grandma said when I laid the yeast on the table. "Did you put the change back in my purse?"

"Yes, grandma," I replied, and hurried out to the porch. I hadn't really lied to grandma, I argued with myself. I did put back all the change I had. But I had spent two pennies without permission. The second piece of candy in my pocket didn't sound like a good idea anymore. I knew I had deceived grandma, and I was miserable about it.

Later that morning, Uncle Roy came to the house for a glass of cold tea. He sat down beside me on the steps.

"Well, what have you been doing with yourself this morning?"

"I went to the store for grandma. And since then I've just been sitting here."

Uncle Roy looked down at me shrewdly. "Something on your mind, is there?"

"I guess so. I'm thinking it over," I replied slowly.

"If there's something you should tell your grandma, I'd advise you to get busy and do it." He chuckled as he got up to leave. "Chances are she knows about it anyway, and the kinder she is to you, the more miserable you'll be."

I watched Uncle Roy make his way back to the barn. He was right. Grandma loved me so much that I couldn't bear to keep anything from her.

While grandma took the hot rolls from the oven, I told her about the candy. She nodded when I finished my story.

"I know just how you feel," she said. "We all feel like that when we've done something deceitful. God is so good to us that we can't help but feel bad when we disobey him. I'm glad you told me about the pennies, and of course I'll forgive you." Grandma hugged me tight, and suddenly I felt as though a big lump was gone from my stomach.

"I guess I should tell you about the time I took something that wasn't mine," grandma said. "I was a pretty sad little girl, too, before it was straightened out." She buttered a roll for me, and we sat down at the table while grandma told her story. . . .

I was still in the primary row at school, which was the first row of seats in our schoolroom. When the different classes recited, the boys and girls came to the front of the room and sat on benches. A lot of the time when I had finished my numbers or letters, I listened to the older ones read or talk about geography.

One day I happened to be watching when one of the big boys stood up to recite. A slate pencil dropped out of his back pocket and rolled under the bench, but he didn't hear it. I was sure he would miss it when he sat down, and begin to look for it. But he didn't. The class finished reciting and went back to their seats, and the pencil stayed there.

I wanted that pencil. We only had a new one once a year, and I thought it would be a good idea to have another in reserve. I knew that it was wrong to steal, but if I happened to find something, surely that was all right.

After a few minutes, I slipped out of my seat, picked up the slate pencil, and quickly put it under my pinafore. The rest of the day I kept telling myself that I had found it, so it was mine.

That evening we sat around the table after supper. Reuben and Roy were doing their homework, and I pulled the pencil out of my pocket to write on my slate. Roy's sharp eyes didn't miss anything.

"Where did you get that new pencil, Mabel?"

"I found it." I glanced at ma to see if she had heard. Of course she had.

"Where did you find it?" she asked me.

"Oh, around school," I replied. I lowered my head and didn't look at the family.

"Did you ask who lost it?" ma persisted.

I shook my head.

"You must do that," ma said. "If no one claims what you find, then you may keep it. But you have to try to find the owner."

I kept my head down, but I nodded to show

ma I understood. What would she think if she found out that I knew who the pencil belonged to?

The evening seemed to stretch out a long time before pa reached for the Bible to have prayer. As he often did, this evening he read from Proverbs. I was busy thinking about how I might continue to keep the pencil if I asked only a few children I knew hadn't lost it, when suddenly I heard what pa was reading. "He who makes a fortune by telling lies runs needlessly into the toils of death."

I didn't understand all that meant, but I knew what a fortune was, and I certainly understood telling lies. To have these things mentioned as running into death caused me to think. I hadn't lied, had I? No, but I had kept back the truth, and I knew ma considered one as bad as the other.

All at once the slate pencil didn't seem like such a treasure to me.

"Ma," I blurted out, "I know who the pencil belongs to."

Roy looked at me with horror. "You mean you *stole* it?"

I began to cry, and pa took me on his lap. "Suppose you tell us all about it, Mabel."

As best I could, I told them about finding the pencil, and even about my plans to keep it. I was sobbing harder with each word I spoke.

"Don't cry, Mabel," pa said as he hugged me tighter. "God is ready to forgive us when we are sorry we've done wrong. Would you like to ask him to forgive you?"

"Yes," I said, and I knew I would be forgiven. The hardest part was to take the pencil back and ask the big boy to forgive me. But it was worth it to have a clear conscience. . . ."

Grandma went back to work, and I thought about her story. I agreed. It was a good feeling to be forgiven.

13

What Shall We Write About?

I HAD JUST FINISHED reading a particularly intriguing story to grandma about a wonderful secret garden and a little girl about my age.

"Oh!" I sighed. "I wish I could write stories like that. Wouldn't that be fun?"

"Yes," grandma replied, "it certainly would. Why don't you try it?"

"Nothing exciting ever happens to me!" I exclaimed. "There certainly aren't any secret gardens around here. What could I write about?"

Grandma laughed. "I'm not sure I could tell

you what to write about, but I could tell you what *not* to write about! I almost wrote about something I shouldn't once."

"Tell me, grandma. What was it?"

Grandma leaned back in her chair and dropped her sewing in her lap. . . .

We didn't have many books to read when I was young, and even in the books at school, there weren't many stories just for entertainment like you have today. But once in a while we would get a newspaper or magazine that had a story in it. Sarah Jane and I would almost memorize the few there were, then we'd make up more after the story ended.

Finally one day, Sarah Jane said, "We ought to write these stories down, Mabel. We could probably even sell them."

"Sell them!" I scoffed. "Who would buy a story we could write?"

"My ma would," Sarah Jane replied. "And yours, too. And my aunt, and maybe Mrs. Hobbs, and the teacher. . . ."

"We still need something to write about," I said. "We don't know very much that's interesting."

"We can make something up. You think about it tonight, and so will I. Then tomorrow we'll write one."

I thought about it all right. I even asked ma, "What do you like to read about?"

Ma thought for a moment. "Well, I like stories about interesting things people do, and I like to read about the lives of people I've heard of. I guess I like biographies."

I pondered that, and decided I didn't know much about the life of anyone important. Everyday happenings on the farm didn't seem too interesting, and the lives of the people I knew were uneventful. That might have ended my writing career, except for the idea Sarah Jane came up with the next day.

Before breakfast, she appeared at our door.

"You're certainly out early this morning, Sarah Jane," ma said. "Have you had your breakfast already?"

"Yes, thank you. Mabel and I have something important to do this morning, so I wanted to get started right away. Is she ready yet?"

"She's still dressing," ma said. "Go on up to her room if you like. But she'll have to eat breakfast before you go out to play."

Sarah Jane burst into my room and closed the door behind her. "I've got it, Mabel! I've got it right here!"

"You've got what?" I asked. Since I hadn't been awake very long, I thought I had missed something.

"Our story!" Sarah Jane exclaimed. "I've got our story!" She pulled a leather-covered book out from under her pinafore.

I stared at it stupidly. "What is it?"

"It's a diary, my cousin Laura's diary. She left it here the last time she visited. She hasn't said anything about it, so she probably doesn't want it anymore."

"But would she want you to read it?" I asked doubtfully. "I don't think she'd like it if we wrote a story about her diary."

"We wouldn't use the same names, silly, just the things that happened. And some of them are really good!"

I was horrified. "You mean you've read your cousin's diary?"

"Well, not *much*," Sarah Jane confessed uncomfortably, "just a few little things. Anyway, if she hadn't wanted anyone to read it, why didn't she take better care of it? Or at least ask us to send it to her?"

I still felt it might be wrong, but Sarah Jane's arguments seemed sound. And ma had said she liked to read about things people did. Sarah Jane's cousin was a person, wasn't she? We agreed to begin our story as soon as I had finished breakfast.

"What are you girls going to do today?" ma asked. "You seem to be in a dreadful hurry to get started. Slow down, Mabel, you'll choke."

"We're going to write a story," Sarah Jane replied. "A story about a young lady who lives in the city."

Ma laughed. "You two don't know much about ladies who live in the city, do you?"

"No," Sarah Jane said, "but we will when we finish reading her . . ." Sarah Jane stopped abruptly and seemed confused.

Ma looked at us closely. "You're not reading someone else's letters, are you? That wouldn't be right, you know."

"Oh, no," I said quickly. "We're not going to read anyone's letters."

"Good," ma replied. "I wouldn't like to think that you would pry into someone's personal affairs."

Ma left the kitchen, and Sarah Jane and I looked at each other.

"Well, it isn't a *letter*," I said.

"No," Sarah Jane agreed. "Besides, finders keepers, losers weepers. I found it, so it belongs to me. What I do with that diary is my business."

I continued to eat my breakfast. I didn't feel good about what we were going to do, but I didn't want Sarah Jane to be upset with me, either.

"Hurry up, Mabel," Sarah Jane urged. "Can't you eat any faster than that?"

Finally I made up my mind. I couldn't do

something I felt was wrong, even to please my best friend.

"Listen, Sarah Jane, maybe that diary isn't a letter, but I don't think your cousin wrote it for anyone else to see. Do you think it would really be honest for us to read it?"

Sarah Jane turned the little book over in her hands. "No, I guess it wouldn't. It is a personal affair, isn't it?"

I nodded, relieved that she had decided that way. Then a thought occurred to me. "What about the stuff you've already looked at?"

"It wasn't very interesting," Sarah Jane confessed. "I saw one day, and it said she washed her hair and had ice cream."

I considered that news for a moment. "We do more exciting things than that right here. How about the day we dressed up the pig and scared Mrs. Carter into hysterics?"

Sarah Jane laughed. "That's right. That was more exciting. But I don't think anyone will buy that story, because everyone already knows it. Maybe we should just take our dolls down to the creek and have a tea party. We might think of another story later."

I agreed, and that ended our story-writing career. I don't think we ever did get back to it. But we learned that an idea for a story shouldn't come from someone else's private business.

14

The Cover-up

THE PARLOR IN GRANDMA'S old home was a special room, saved for company. It wasn't often used by the family, so there were rules for it that didn't apply to the rest of the house. One was "We don't eat in the parlor."

I knew this rule and had not thought of disobeying it. But one day as I munched on a cookie in the kitchen, I happened to think of a picture in the photograph album that I wanted to see. Still holding the cookie, I went into the parlor. I was turning the pages of the album when I heard grandma coming down the hall. Quickly I pushed the cookie down between the chair and the cushion. I intended to go back and get it, but during the course of the day, I forgot about it.

The next time grandma cleaned the parlor, she found the dried-out cookie crumbs.

"I'm sorry, grandma," I said. "I didn't mean to take it in there. I just forgot."

"Why in the world did you shove it down in the chair?" she asked.

"I thought you'd scold me."

"Well, I would have. And I should now. You know better than to cover up something you've done wrong. You can be pretty sure it will be found out."

Uncle Roy came into the kitchen just then, and he began to laugh.

"I don't see anything very funny about that, Roy," grandma said. "I'm trying to teach the child to be obedient."

"I'm not laughing at what she did. I just remembered something *I* covered up. Do you remember the time I teased you about the dishes, Mabel?"

"Oh, my, I should say so. I hadn't thought about that for a long time. That certainly proved that your sin will surely find you out."

Of course I had to know all about that, so grandma told me the story. . . .

I was only about six when it happened. I

wanted to help ma with the work, and I begged her to let me do the dishes. She wasn't sure that I could handle the whole job, but she would let me wash and dry the silverware occasionally.

One evening as ma started to wash the supper dishes, I began to pester her to let me do them. Roy was in the kitchen, and I guess he decided this would be a good time to tease me.

"You're too little, Mabel," he said. "You know you can't do dishes; that's not a job for babies. Wait until you get big like me."

"I can so!" I retorted. "I'm not a baby, and I can do dishes as well as you can!"

"Oh, no! You can't do *anything* as well as I can. You're still a baby. And besides, you're just a girl!"

This was more than I could stand, and I lit into Roy with both fists. I was howling with rage, and Roy was laughing at my attempts to pound him. Ma decided she had heard enough.

"Mabel, stop that right now," she commanded. "And Roy, since you're so big, and a boy, you can do the dishes tonight."

This was certainly not what Roy had planned on. "Aw, no, ma! I didn't mean it! She can do the dishes if she wants to."

"You can do the dishes, whether you want to or not," ma said firmly. "Maybe you'll learn not to tease your sister so much."

So she tied an apron around Roy's middle and told him to get busy. He did, but he grumbled loudly. Ma ignored him and took me into the other room. I didn't find out what happened until I was much older.

After ma and I left the kitchen, Roy began to pile the dishes into the dishpan. Ma was always very careful to put just a few dishes in at a time. But Roy was anxious to have this distasteful job over, so he dumped most of them in together.

He soon wished he hadn't for he reached into the dishpan and took out *half* of one of ma's good plates. He fished around in the pan and found the other half. He thought maybe he could mend it before ma found out, so he would put the two pieces out by the hen house to glue them in the morning.

His intentions were good, but his judgment wasn't. Without bothering to dry his soapy hands, he started out the back door with the broken plate. Partway down the path, it began to slip from his grasp. Unable to hold one piece and grab for the other, Roy watched them both fall to the ground and smash into small bits!

He glanced back at the door. No one had heard what happened, so he pushed the pieces into the grass beside the path. He figured he could get up early and pick them up before ma saw them, and if she missed the plate before then, he'd just have to tell her he broke it.

Roy returned to the kitchen, and working more carefully, finished the dishes. As the boys went up to bed that night, Roy asked Reuben to wake him up early.

"What for?" Reuben asked suspiciously. "You never want to get up early."

"Well, tomorrow I do. And that's none of your business."

The next morning Roy was awakened early to discover that it had snowed during the night. There was no sign of a path between the house and the barnyard. He breathed a sigh of relief as he realized that he couldn't pick up the pieces now, and no one would see them. He promptly dismissed the broken plate from his mind and didn't think about it again.

That winter happened to be one of the stormiest we had. The snow didn't leave the ground at all. New snow fell before the old could melt. But spring came, as it always does, and one morning pa came in for breakfast with some news.

"I think I saw one of your good plates this morning," he said to ma.

"A plate! Where did you see it?"

"It's out there beside the path," pa replied. "But it's in too many pieces to do you much good. Did you forget that you broke it?"

"No, I certainly did not. I wouldn't forget

something like that. And I don't remember anyone else saying they had, either." Ma looked directly at me.

"Not me," I said quickly. "I didn't break it. Honest, ma."

"I did," Roy admitted in a small voice.

"You!" ma exclaimed. "When did you have my good plate outside?"

"The night you made me wash the dishes. It was an accident. I didn't mean to break it."

Ma looked puzzled. "Why in the world didn't you say something about it before?"

"I meant to fix it," Roy said. "But it snowed and covered it up, and I forgot all about it. I'm sorry."

Pa looked at Roy sternly. "I hope you're sorry you broke the plate, and not just sorry the snow melted. You should have told ma about it right away. You know that what you cover up will be found out sooner or later, don't you?"

Roy nodded and looked ashamed.

"You can save your money and buy a new plate. And remember," pa added more kindly, "even if your parents never find out what you do, God knows about it and you are responsible to him. . . ."

Uncle Roy nodded as grandma finished the

story. "I didn't forget that," he said. "I've tried to live my life so the Lord would be pleased with me. I sure know it's useless to cover up anything!"

15

The Haircut

ONE OF THE THINGS I liked to do best when I was a little girl was to brush grandma's hair. Sometimes just before bedtime, when she took her hair down for the night, I had the chance to do that. The big bone hairpins were carefully placed in the little china dish on her dresser, and all her beautiful, long hair would fall down her back.

"I never saw such long hair, grandma," I said one evening. "Haven't you ever had it cut?"

Grandma handed me the brush and picked up her sewing. "You could almost say that," she laughed. "It was never all cut off short, but some of it did get cut once."

"Tell me about it," I begged. "How did it happen? Did you get in trouble for it?"

"I was in trouble, all right," grandma replied. "But not so much for the cut hair as for what I did to cover it up."

Grandma thought for a moment, then began her story. . . .

It was a dark rainy day. Sarah Jane and I were playing in the upstairs rooms until the rain stopped, and we could go outside. Sarah Jane had come over early that morning to show me a birthday gift she had received the day before. I was suitably impressed, because I had never had anything that nice. It was a beautiful, heart-shaped locket.

"What are you going to put in it?" I asked. "You'll have to have something special for that pretty locket."

Sarah Jane nodded. "I know. I'd like to have a nice picture." She looked at me thoughtfully. "You're my best friend. Do you have a picture I could put in here?"

I shook my head. "I am afraid not. All the pictures of me are in the big album downstairs. If one was missing, ma would notice right away."

Sarah Jane sighed. "It's a shame not to have something to put in it." Then she brightened. "My cousin has a piece of hair in her locket. You have lots of curls. Maybe I could have one to put in mine."

I was pleased that Sarah Jane wanted to put something that belonged to me in her locket, but I wasn't really sure about the hair.

"I don't know," I said. "I don't think ma would like it. I've never had my hair cut."

"She won't even see it," Sarah Jane insisted. "I'll cut it out from underneath."

"Well, be careful. I don't want to get into trouble."

I ran to get the scissors, then sat down on the footstool, and Sarah Jane went to work. She lifted up the top curls and chose one underneath to cut.

"This is a good one. All the others cover this spot. I'll only cut a little bit off the end, and you can see how it looks. Maybe you'd like some cut off every curl."

"Oh, I don't think so," I said quickly. "One will be enough. I'll be in trouble if ma sees that much gone."

"Don't worry," Sarah Jane said. "I'm not going to hurt it."

She picked up the scissors and began to snip the end off the curl. Just at that moment, a door slammed downstairs and both of us jumped. The scissors closed on my hair, and three curls dropped to the floor!

"Oh! Look what you did! How am I ever going to cover up all those curls?"

"I couldn't help it," Sarah Jane said. "You shouldn't have jumped."

"Well, you jumped, too. How did I know you had half my hair in your hand? You said just one curl!"

"The rest of them fell down in the way when you moved," she said. "I couldn't help it." I ran to the mirror and looked at my hair.

"Oh," I moaned, "wait until ma sees that. I'm really going to get it this time."

Sarah Jane looked remorseful. "Maybe you can comb it some other way so it won't be noticed."

"Ma always combs my hair. There's no way to keep her from seeing it."

"You could put your sunbonnet on," Sarah Jane suggested. "That would cover it up."

"I guess I could," I said doubtfully. "Maybe I can think of someway to tell her before she sees it."

I ran to get my sunbonnet and tucked my hair up underneath it. No one would see what had happened until I had to take it off.

"Won't your ma wonder why you're wearing a sunbonnet when it's raining?" Sarah Jane asked when I returned.

"You're the one who suggested it," I said crossly. "And you're the one who cut my hair off. Now you can just pray that the sun comes out."

Whether she did or not, I don't know; but very shortly the rain stopped, and the sun came out. We hurried as far away from the house as possible for the rest of the morning.

When dinner time approached, I had to think of some way to stay away from ma.

"Sarah Jane, why don't you run up to the house and ask ma if we can have some sandwiches for a picnic?"

"Oh, I can't," Sarah Jane said. "I promised ma I'd be home by dinner time. I'll have to hurry now, or I'll be late. I'll try to come back this afternoon."

I sat on a rock and watched Sarah Jane run across the field. There was no need for her to rush back, I thought glumly. There probably wouldn't be anything left of me to visit.

I sat there as long as I dared. I knew ma would send one of the boys to find me if I didn't come when the dinner bell rang the second time, so I trudged slowly toward the house, hoping against hope that ma would be too busy to notice me. I arrived at the door just as everyone sat down at the table.

Ma glanced at me and said, "I thought you'd gone home with Sarah Jane. Hurry and wash.

We're ready to eat now."

I dawdled with the washing as long as possible, then slipped into my chair. Pa asked the blessing, and ma began to dish up the food.

"Haven't you forgotten something, Mabel?" pa asked.

"No, I don't think so, pa."

"You've still got your bonnet on, silly," said Roy.

"Oh, that," I said quickly. "I'm going right back out after dinner. I thought I'd save time by not having to put it on again."

I bent my head over my plate and began to eat quickly. Since no one said anything, I ventured to look up. Everyone was looking at me in a strange way. Roy continued to stuff food into his mouth while keeping his eyes on me, but the others had stopped eating. I put my head down again.

"Mabel," said ma, "is there something you ought to tell us?"

"Oh, no, ma. It's just that Sarah Jane will be back after dinner, and we are doing something special down by the brook."

That would not have been the end of the matter, I am sure, except that at just that moment our neighbor, Mr. Hobbs, drove into the yard. Pa went out to meet him, and ma hurried to set another place at the table. With a sigh of relief, I continued my dinner.

Mr. Hobbs came in and sat down, and after a few words with pa about the crops, he said, "Well, Jim, do you have a young lady visiting you today?"

"This is just me, Mr. Hobbs," I said.

"Oh, so it is!" Mr. Hobbs exclaimed. "Why, with that fancy bonnet, I was sure it must be a fine lady from town."

Ma returned to the table with more food, and she looked at me with disgust. "Mabel, go take off that sunbonnet. You look ridiculous."

"I'm through eating now, ma," I said. "Couldn't I please go outside?"

If Mr. Hobbs had not been there, ma would have insisted that I obey her. But since he was, and I had finished my dinner, she allowed me to leave. Thankfully I ran back to the brook to wait for Sarah Jane. Finally she arrived, breathless, and dropped into the grass.

"What did your ma say?" she asked.

"She doesn't know yet. I didn't take off my bonnet. I was just lucky Mr. Hobbs came." And I told Sarah Jane what had happened.

She sat up and looked at me in amazement. "Now you will be in for it. I've found that no matter how bad you are, you end up being twice as bad if you hide it from your folks. My ma always says, 'Be sure your sin will find you out,' and it always does."

"Well, you're not much comfort," I retorted. "It's easy for you to say that, since it isn't your hair that's cut off."

"Take off your bonnet, and let's see it again," Sarah Jane said. "Maybe it doesn't look as bad as we thought it did."

I pulled off my sunbonnet, and Sarah Jane gazed at my tangled curls.

"It looks as bad as we thought it did," she said dismally. "I don't know how you're going to cover it up."

"It's a sure thing I can't go around wearing my sunbonnet until it grows out. I won't get away with that again. You'll have to think of something else."

"*I* will!" Sarah Jane cried. "It's *your* hair—" Then she stopped. "I guess you're right. It was my fault for wanting to put a curl in my locket. The only thing to do is go tell your ma what happened, and let her punish me, too." She sighed. "When do you want to do it?"

"I won't have any fun sitting here thinking about it all afternoon," I replied glumly. "We might as well go now."

Slowly I replaced my bonnet, and Sarah Jane and I started for the house.

"What do you think she'll do?" Sarah Jane asked. "Will she spank us?"

I considered that for a moment. "No, I don't think so. Ma doesn't spank me very often, and she wouldn't ever spank you. It will be something worse than that. We probably won't be able to play together for a long time."

Ma was sitting on the porch, shelling peas for supper. As we approached, she looked up and smiled. "Did you girls have a nice time at the brook?" she asked. "I thought you'd be back up to the house before you went home, Sarah Jane. You forgot something."

Ma pulled Sarah Jane's locket and my curls from her apron pocket!

We gazed at them in silence. This was not at all what we had expected.

"I hope you've learned something today, girls," ma said. "The hurting of your own uneasy conscience is worse than any punishment anyone else can give you."

She looked at my sunbonnet. "Covering something up doesn't make it go away. You knew I would see what had happened sooner or later, didn't you, Mabel?"

I nodded miserably.

"Well, come on," ma said kindly. "Let's wash your hair and see if we can part it on the other side until that place grows out. I think you've suffered enough. We won't have to let pa and the boys know what happened. . . ."

"And that's what we did," grandma said.

"Sarah Jane and I never forgot that lesson. Fortunately, hair grows back again. Everything isn't that easily repaired, however."

"And did Sarah Jane get the curl for her locket?" I asked.

"Oh, yes," Grandma laughed. "Ma let her keep it. But she really didn't need it to remember me or that day."

16

Grandma Makes a Friend

GRANDMA WAS GETTING ready to prepare some corn for supper when I came into the kitchen and plopped down on a chair. I reached for an ear of corn and viciously pulled off the husks.

"I hate that mean old Tommy Rice," I said.

Grandma looked at me in surprise. "You hate him? Surely you don't mean that."

"Well, I do. You don't know what he did today."

"No, I don't. But it couldn't be anything bad enough to make you hate him. Do you know what the Bible says about hating your brother?"

"He's not *my* brother," I muttered, but I knew that the Bible meant any other person when it said *brother*.

Grandma ignored that comment and reached for her Bible. She quickly turned to the place she wanted and handed it to me. "Why don't you read this verse?" She pointed to the fifteenth verse of the third chapter of 1 John.

"For every one who hates his brother is a murderer, and no murderer as you know, has eternal life within him."

"A murderer!" I said. "I don't hate him *that* much. I just don't like him—not one little bit."

Grandma nodded her head. "I can understand that. We're not likely to think much of people who are mean to us. But the Bible tells us what we can do about that, too."

"It does? . . . What does it say?"

"It says to love your enemies and pray for those that despitefully use you."

I thought about that for a moment. "That's a pretty hard thing to ask someone to do. I guess I could pray for Tommy, but I know I'd never love him!"

Grandma laughed. "You'd be surprised. It's awfully hard to dislike someone when you really pray for them. In fact, the person you pray for could turn out to be one of your best friends. That happened to me once."

"I want to hear about that," I said, so while I pulled strings of silk from the corn, grandma began the story. . . .

It was the year I was in the third reader at school. My best friend Sarah Jane and I had shared a desk all through the years, and, of course, we shared everything else, too. Then one morning I arrived at school to find someone else sitting on my side of the desk.

Miss Gibson was our teacher that year. She saw how surprised I looked. "Mabel, this is Alice. She is going to be here for the rest of the year. I didn't think you'd mind sitting in the extra seat so she wouldn't be alone."

Alice smiled at me, and right away I knew I didn't like her. I *did* mind giving up my seat, but I couldn't tell Miss Gibson that.

"Why don't you tell Miss Gibson that you don't want me to be moved?" I whispered to Sarah Jane as soon as I had the chance.

"I told her," Sarah Jane whispered back. "But she said she didn't think you'd care."

All morning I watched as Sarah Jane helped Alice find the place in the book, or showed her where to sit when we recited. The more I watched, the unhappier I became, and the less I liked Alice.

At recess they walked around the school

yard together and talked to the other girls. When I could get Sarah Jane off by herself, I let her know how I felt.

"You like that new girl better than you do me," I stormed. "You've forgotten all about being my friend."

Sarah Jane looked hurt. "Why, no I haven't, Mabel. You know I'd never forget that we're best friends. I have to be nice to Alice because she's new and doesn't know anyone."

I tossed my head and turned up my nose. "I don't have to be nice to her, and I won't either. She has no business coming here and taking my place."

I stalked off before Sarah Jane could reply, and at lunch time I ate by myself, even though the girls urged me to eat with them.

As the days went by, I continued to snub Alice and be irritable with Sarah Jane. I had to admire the new girl, though. She was so pretty, with delicate features and long, shiny curls. I had curls, too, but I was definitely not delicate. And to make matters worse, Alice wore fluffy dresses with big sashes—it seemed like a new one every day. The contrast between her dresses and the plain ones with pinafores that I wore was almost more than I could stand.

One morning after Alice had been there for several weeks, I decided to change matters. I appeared at the breakfast table in my best Sunday dress.

"Where in the world are you going?" ma asked.

"To school," I replied haughtily.

"Not in that dress," ma said decidedly.

"But, ma . . ." I began.

"No buts," she replied firmly. "Back to your room and put on your school dress. Then come here and let me tie your ribbon."

"She wants to look like the new girl," Roy snickered. "Alice wears a Sunday dress every day."

"Well, Mabel doesn't," ma said. "I have better things to do than iron fancy dresses."

I glared at Roy, but I had no choice but to change my dress. I had already started the day off badly, and I was hardly surprised when it kept getting worse.

Almost the first thing I did at school was to fall over Alice's feet as I carried some books to the front of the room. The books flew every way, and, of course, the children laughed.

"She put her foot out there on purpose," I complained loudly.

"Oh, I'm sure she didn't," Miss Gibson said. "It was just an accident. Let's not even think about it again." She patted me on the back.

Maybe Miss Gibson didn't think about it again, but I certainly did. The longer I thought, the more convinced I was that Alice had deliberately tried to humiliate me. I rushed home after school to tell ma the story.

"She did that on purpose to embarrass me, and I'll never forgive her for it, not ever!" I meant it, too. But that evening at family prayer, pa read some verses that sounded as though they had been written just for me.

"And when you stand praying, if you have a grievance against anyone, forgive him, so that your Father in heaven may forgive the wrongs you have done."

I looked at ma, but she was listening, and didn't act as though she remembered what I had said. I was ashamed, and when it was my turn to pray, I asked the Lord to bless Alice. I felt better that night than I had anytime since she had been at school.

The next morning, ma put some extra cookies in my lunch pail. "To share with your friends," she said.

I knew what she meant. And from that day on I began to find out what a lovely girl Alice really was. She became one of my best friends that year. I guess nobody really wants enemies. . . .

Grandma gathered up the corn to put it on the stove, and I wandered out to the barn to look for Uncle Roy. Grandma was right, I thought. And you don't have to have enemies either. If you pray for them, they turn into friends!